HANNAH'S STORY

My heart beat faster as the pounding boots came closer. Then it was quiet: the boots had halted outside our door. "Open up!" came a hoarse voice accompanied by hammering at the door...

ESCAPE FROM WAR

HANNAH'S STORY

READ FRANK·FIRST THEN READ HANNAH

KINGFISHER
An imprint of Kingfisher Publications Plc
New Penderel House, 283–288 High Holborn
London WC1V 7HZ
www.kingfisherpub.com

First published by Kingfisher 2005
This edition published by Kingfisher 2006
2 4 6 8 10 9 7 5 3 1

A CIP catalogue record for this book
is available from the British Library.

ISBN-13: 978 0 7534 1354 8
ISBN-10: 0 7534 1354 X

Printed in India
1TR/0206/THOM/SGCH/80STORA/C

MY SIDE OF THE STORY

ESCAPE FROM WAR

HANNAH'S STORY

JAMES RIORDAN

KINGFISHER

Have you read Frank's side of the story?
If you haven't, flip back and read it first; if you
have, you can now read Hannah's side of the story!

Chapter One

It was coming from a long way off, *bang-bang-bang*, like hammer blows at a smithy.

It woke me up and at first I thought it was part of a dream. But my dream faded the moment I opened my eyes. Still the pounding went on.

As I raised my head from the pillow, I realized the noise was drifting up from the street. It now sounded like an army of soldiers marching in rhythm, tramping over the cobblestones, coming closer and closer and closer. I switched on the light and glanced at the alarm clock. It was just after one o'clock.

Had war started? Was the army marching through Hamburg on its way to Poland or Russia? With Hitler, you could never tell where he'd strike next.

But other noises confused me. Soldiers marched, they sometimes sang and, like those in red jackets and shiny brass helmets at the park bandstand, they made music – blowing trumpets and trombones, clashing cymbals and banging drums. But this was more like a rabble: shouting, yelling, bawling, as if drunk or crazed in some way. And there were other, more frightening sounds: babies howling, women shrieking, men screaming. I distinctly heard a woman sobbing and crying, *"No! No! No!"*

The screams mingled with sounds of breaking glass — as if hooligans were smashing windows.

I jumped out of bed, shaking with fright. In my bare feet I ran to the window overlooking the main street. We were on the fourth floor, so I had a clear view of the roadway below.

In the light of gas lamps and despite the frosty night, I could see groups of men, some in black, some in the brown shirts of storm troopers. They wore peaked caps and big leather gloves, and held what looked like heavy crow bars in their hands. One group was busy smashing up Dr Askenase's surgery in the next block. Another was breaking the windows of Uncle Jakob's corner shop, scattering his pipes and tins of tobacco all over the pavement.

Then I saw Uncle Jakob, running up and down in his nightshirt, begging the attackers to stop. I watched in horror as a youth following the brown-shirted mob started hitting him from behind with a lump of wood, until he stumbled and collapsed in the middle of the road.

"About time they got what's coming to them!" someone shouted.

"Come away from the window, Hannah!" Papa's angry voice startled me. He and Mama were already up. Mama was checking the front door, while Papa was carrying a pile of papers from his desk to the wardrobe in my room.

"Get back to bed," he whispered.

Hans was helping Papa with the papers.

"I don't think the Nazis will touch people's homes," Papa was saying to no one in particular. "They're just running amok through the streets, smashing the windows of Jewish shops and businesses. But I'd best hide my papers… to be on the safe side."

He couldn't have been more wrong. Though I pulled the covers over my head to try to shut out the racket, I could still hear boots tramping along the street and stopping at the main door of our apartment block. Then, someone banged on the outside door and, finding it locked, tried to break it down.

Hurriedly, Mama put out all the lights before she, Papa and Hans huddled in one corner of the main bedroom. We all kept as quiet as little mice.

I could hear hobnailed boots tramping up the stairs, gruff voices barking orders, the noise of splintering wood as doors were broken. The squads must have had a list of addresses because only certain apartments were being searched.

That meant they were bound to come for us!

My heart beat faster and faster as the pounding boots came closer and closer. Then, for one agonizing moment, it was quiet: the boots had halted outside our door.

"Open up!" came a hoarse voice accompanied by hammering at the door. We held our breath. I don't know whether they had axes, but they started smashing down the door. In next to no time, they'd burst in and switched on all the lights. They rushed about, hitting out at anything in their way.

I slid further under the bedclothes, shivering in terror. Next thing I knew, the bedclothes were ripped off and I was yanked from bed to floor.

There were eight of them, like mad dogs, their faces twisted with hate. While I stood shaking, hastily pulling on clothes over my nightdress, four of the men, all wearing red swastika armbands, started searching the wardrobe and scattering papers and books all over the floor.

That done, they then set to toppling the heavy wardrobe – "One, two, three!" – I was terrified! If it fell on me, it would crush every bone in my body! The wardrobe fell. It came crashing down, but, suddenly, as I was about to scream, one side caught on the bedside table, leaving a small space underneath. That space saved my life. I kept as still as I could, holding my breath.

The men must have thought I was crushed to

death, for they left the bedroom, and I could hear them smashing furniture, chandeliers and pictures in the living room. Papa's stern voice rose above the row. "Please leave us in peace. I am a musician, not a shopkeeper."

The fallen wardrobe had trapped my left foot and, after the initial shock, it was starting to hurt badly. I couldn't help myself: I let out a loud groan which I desperately tried to stifle with my fist. Too late. One of the men must have heard it, for he came rushing back in, cursing and dragging me out from under the wardrobe.

Pulling me roughly by the arm, he forced me into the living room and pushed me towards my parents. Hans was nowhere to be seen.

Mama's precious crystal and Meissen porcelain were strewn in pieces all over the floor. The intruders had smashed everything breakable – cups, saucers, plates, bowls. Even then they weren't satisfied. One spotty youth snatched from the sideboard Mama's heavy nine-branched candle-holder, the menorah, and wielded it like a club.

Perhaps remembering Papa's words, another youth disappeared into the next room, emerging triumphantly while brandishing the valuable Stradivarius violin.

"So! You're a fiddler, are you?" he said with a grin. "How'd you like to give us a tune?" Papa looked down, slowly shaking his head.

"What? You won't?"

The man suddenly grabbed me by the arm, twisting it behind my back. I let out a yell of pain, much to the brute's delight.

"Sorry," I murmured. "I didn't mean to, Papa."

"Let her go," he said calmly. "She's only ten. I'll play."

The man let go of my arm and held out Papa's violin. But before he could take it the man dropped it on the floor and stamped on it, breaking the priceless violin into several pieces and making the broken strings twang like a tinny piano.

"Oh dear! Butterfingers!" he said to Papa with a grin. "You dropped it and I accidentally trod on it. What a shame!"

Papa's face flushed with anger. For a moment I thought he was going to strike the leering brute. But he controlled himself, no doubt mindful of what might happen if he did anything silly. Mama gently took his arm.

When there was nothing left to break, the storm trooper leader yelled at us, "Put on your hats and coats and come with us."

We followed them dumbly on to the street —
Mama, Papa and me. Where had Hans got to?

Outside we joined a column of people being led
to the main square at the end of the road. We saw lots
and lots of people we knew. Many were crying.
Some had evidently been dragged out of hospital
beds: the old, the infirm, some hardly able to walk.
Those men not walking fast enough for their
tormentors were being pulled along by their beards.
One woman fell over   fainted or dead, I couldn't
tell. In the cold and dark of that November night, it
was very frightening.

In the far corner of the square stood the old
synagogue. Flames and smoke were swirling up from
its roof and windows, and storm troopers were
chucking out prayer books to be gathered in a heap
and burned. The old Rabbi was being jerked about by
his beard like a billy goat until blood flowed. They
then made him dance upon the burning books.

I kept as close to Mama and Papa as I could. My
crushed foot was so painful I thought it must be
broken. Papa picked me up and cradled me in his
arms, whispering, "Try to bear it, little one. And don't
worry about your brother. He's shivering on the
balcony where he hid when they burst in."

When the flames from the burning books had died

11

down, buckets were fetched and the synagogue elders were made to shovel up the ashes. Then, as the uniformed men laughed, the old men were forced to scrub the square clean of scorch marks.

Chapter Two

By now it was the middle of the night and I was feeling very tired, resting my head on Papa's shoulder. I wondered when the Nazis would let us go home. But they had other plans.

We were herded from the square like cattle and driven with blows to an old cinema. As we went in, a tall, thin man in glasses was issuing orders in a shrill voice, "Men at the front, women and children at the back!"

Papa put me down, kissed Mama and me, and walked slowly towards the front-row seats.

The bespectacled commander seemed to be waiting for further orders. Either that or he didn't know what to do with us. As the hours dragged by, some of the storm troopers appeared to grow bored. They started calling men from the front rows up to the stage. I spotted Papa and Uncle Jakob, his head covered by a bloodstained bandage.

What were they going to do with them? I felt so afraid for Papa, knowing how short-tempered he was. What if they made him sing? Being a musician didn't mean he had a good singing voice; that might not please the captors.

Some twenty men were lined up to one side of the

stage while a youth arranged chairs and a table in the centre. It looked like they were going to interrogate the prisoners, one by one, in public.

Nothing so civilized. The commander mounted the stage, cracking a whip. Approaching the prisoners, still in their hats and coats, he shouted, "Strip to your underpants!"

The men looked at each other in astonishment. Nobody moved.

With a sharp crack of his whip, the commander repeated the order.

Glancing at each other helplessly, the men muttered among themselves, but did nothing.

A third whiplash, this time on the men's heads and backs, stung some into action.

About half a dozen, Uncle Jakob among them, started undressing. The others looked on in embarrassment.

"Now," said the tall man with a grin, "you will jump over the chair like dogs!"

He cracked his whip, yelling at the nearest man, "Allez-oop!"

It was poor Uncle Jakob. He looked even smaller than usual, standing there, bandy-legged in baggy grey underpants, black socks and boots. He started forward awkwardly, took a run at the chair, but didn't jump high enough. Both he and the chair crashed to the floor.

The 'ringmaster' and his cronies fell about laughing, roaring out, "Higher! Higher! Higher!"

The second man had a long straggly beard, parted in the middle. He was a good twenty years older than Uncle Jakob, his back bent, legs bowed. As he stumbled forward, his pants fell to his ankles and he stopped, quickly covering his shrivelled parts. That set the guards off even more.

"More! More! More!" bawled the tormentors. They were obviously enjoying the 'circus'.

A third man, younger and fatter than the first two, responded to the whip crack by taking a running jump at the chair and clearing it – to cheers from the brown-shirts. But the 'ringmaster' wasn't satisfied.

"You're supposed to jump on to the chair, not over it, ninny! Do it again!"

This time the fat man leapt on to the chair, as ordered. It creaked and swayed under his weight, as he kept his balance by gripping the back of the chair.

"Good doggie!" shouted the commander. "Now, let's see you beg for a biscuit. On to your hind legs! Up! Up! Up!"

The poor man, scared out of his wits, took his hands from the chair and tried to imitate a dog begging. But he lost his balance, fell over backwards and rolled off the stage. Someone rushed forward to help him while the 'circus master' was doubled up with laughter.

"Can't make dogs out of pigs!" he chortled.

The 'show' continued for the amusement of the guards – and the mounting alarm of the audience. I wondered what Papa would do when it was his turn. He was such a proud man. And headstrong.

At last, it came to him. My heart was in my mouth, my hands clammy. I glanced to the side, Mama had hidden her face in her hands. I followed suit, but squinted through my fingers. Part of me wanted Papa to defy the brutes, not to humiliate himself. But part of me was scared of what might happen.

Papa was standing to one side, as if he hadn't heard the order. The whip came whistling down on his head.

"Get your clothes off, Jew pig!" snarled the 'ringmaster'. Papa didn't move.

He just stared into the darkness of the hall as if seeking us out, asking forgiveness for what he was about to do.

The tall man barked no more orders. Presumably he didn't want one rogue dog to spoil the show. Yet he needed to teach him a lesson. Advancing on Papa, he slapped him hard across the face. I could hardly look.

Papa scarcely shook his head. It was as if he could see us, and we were giving him courage.

Another blow. This time it brought blood spurting from his nose. But he just gave a slight shake of the head and stared straight at his attacker. A third blow with a fist knocked him off his feet. But right away he stood up, expressionless.

Enraged by this insolence, the 'ringmaster' now hit Papa about the head until both his eyes were swollen and half-closed, his nose and mouth were streaming blood, and his ears were like raw meat. One final blow with the whip handle knocked him down again. This time he didn't get up.

That brought the 'performance' to an end. The bullies had had their fun, even if Papa had spoiled their finale.

For the rest of the night and morning we were left alone, freezing cold and hungry. Papa was left on the lighted stage in a pool of blood. No one could go to his aid.

Tears streamed down my cheeks and there was nothing Mama could do to console me. First she cursed Papa for his pig-headedness.

"Stubborn as a mule. He'll get all of us killed. Why did he have to annoy them? It's best to do as they say."

Then, after a while, she said softly, "Why aren't there more like my Freddie?" She only called him 'Freddie' on special occasions.

As for me, I felt a tingle of pride run through my whole body. That was my papa lying there. He hadn't given in. He showed them up for what they were: bullies and cowards. I vowed I'd try to be like him, always.

I must have dozed off because when I opened my eyes Papa had gone. There was no one on stage. Just two fallen chairs and a table, and a dark patch. All the men were sitting on cherry plush seats or lying on the floor in the front stalls. It was early afternoon. What had woken me was a sudden clamour in the back rows where we were sitting. Behind us, women and children were filing out of the cinema. Where to now?

"Hurry up!" shouted a broad-shouldered youth, waving a revolver in the air. "Clear the seats!"

Once outside in the frosty November air, we were surprised at the lack of guards. No one to chivvy us into columns or tell us where to go. Could it be all over? We didn't wait to find out.

"Come on, Hannah," said Mama in a half-whisper, as if we might suddenly be stopped. My left foot had gone to sleep and I had to wiggle my toes to get the blood moving again. But the less numb it grew, the more painful it became, especially when I put any weight on the foot.

"Here, take my arm and lean on me," said Mama, tugging me hard. "You're too big for me to carry."

I limped along as best I could, willing to put up with any pain as long as we escaped from the cinema.

"Where's Papa?" I asked, looking back at the dispersing crowd for any sign of him and Uncle Jakob. There were no men to be seen, just a few schoolboys.

"They must be keeping them in, letting people go in dribs and drabs, starting with the back rows."

We trudged home, cold, miserable and starving. We passed the still-smoking ruins of the synagogue, over the shattered plate-glass windows of Jewish stores, trying not to tread on wares left on the cobblestones.

Chapter Three

Waiting for us in the apartment was a terrified party of relatives eager for news: Hans, Uncle Jakob's wife Rachel and son Erich, as well as another aunt and two cousins. No one knew what to do. Aunt Rachel had bought the day's newspaper that reported 'An Outrage'.

But what the 'outrage' referred to was not beatings, burnings or other brutal attacks on innocent Jews. It was the 'justified outrage of Germans' on what the paper called the 'Night of Broken Glass': November the ninth, 1938.

Aunt Rachel unfolded the newspaper and read out the report, 'From an Eye-Witness Correspondent':

The patience of the German Folk was finally broken on Crystal Night. They could no longer stand by as Jewish terrorists gunned down Germans in cold blood.

In Paris, on 7 November, the Polish Jew Herschel Grynszpan broke into the German Embassy and shot the German diplomat Ernst vom Rath. He died of his wounds two days later. On hearing of this atrocity, some young people took revenge, to teach Jews a lesson. Many Jews were arrested.

"So they're calling it 'Crystal Night', are they?" said Mama indignantly.

"What are we going to do?" asked Erich. "What will they do with my father?"

No one had an answer. But the question brought us all back to our immediate dilemma. Everyone had dreadful stories of the night before. My two other cousins claimed they'd seen old men being beaten to death for disobeying orders. I thought of Papa and how lucky he'd been to escape with his life – if he was still alive. Luckily for him he'd been beaten in full view of hundreds of people, not in some dark alleyway.

"Hans, Erich," ordered Mama, "go to the cinema and find out where they took the men. Some may need help."

"Keep your heads down," added Aunt Rachel. "Don't get yourselves arrested."

They were back within the hour. "They were bundled into the back of lorries," said Hans breathlessly. "And driven off."

"When I asked a guard where they were heading," added Erich, "he said to the barracks. For 'processing'."

"What does 'processing' mean?" I asked.

"No idea," answered Mama. "Process? Trial? But what crime have they committed?"

Mama suddenly made up her mind. "I'm going to sort this out," she declared.

"Are you sure that's wise, Grete?" asked Aunt Rachel anxiously.

"Wise or not, I must go," she replied.

"I'll come with you, Mama," I cried.

"No, I'd best go alone. The rest of you can stay here. Don't use or answer the phone... You never know. And Hans, take a look at your sister's foot. If need be, call Dr Askenase."

"If he's still alive," said Hans gloomily.

I knew the army barracks was somewhere on the outskirts of town, between Hamburg and Luneberg Heath, too far for the tram. Mama would be gone for some time.

Everyone was so tired after the worst night of our lives that, having eaten a quick snack, they all went off home, leaving Hans and me alone.

We woke up late. Everything was quiet.

"What if they've thrown her into prison too?" asked Hans, his voice shaking.

Mama eventually returned as it was growing dark. She looked crushed. Gone was her usual dimpled smile that had always given us strength. Her black eyes had dark rings round them and showed uncertainty and fear.

"What did he say?"

"What's going on?"

"When's he coming home?"

She ignored our questions and sank down on a broken chair beside the dining-room table (we'd cleared up most of the mess). Holding her head in her hands, she wept. Not silent tears, not watery sniffs, but loud sobs, her shoulders shaking, her wailing coming in fits and starts, broken only by calls of, "Freddie! Freddie!"

"Best let her be until she's cried it out," said Hans. "Go and make some tea."

Mama was clearly distraught. But, as she sipped her tea, she got out her story.

"They wouldn't let me see him…"

She broke down again, her chest heaving, tears choking her throat. When she had calmed down, she spoke in a whisper, as if afraid someone might overhear.

"At the barracks I heard a soldier say they've built special prisons – 'concentration camps' he called them. At a place called Dachau in the south, and Buchenwald in the east."

"What for, Mama?" I asked in a hushed voice.

"He said they're for troublemakers."

"What are troublemakers?" I asked, puzzled.

"Communists and Jews." It was Hans who provided the answer.

"But Jews don't cause trouble," I said with a sigh.

"The soldier said Jews were ruining Germany," continued Mama. "So Hitler is going to round up their ringleaders and put them somewhere safe, where they won't do any harm – sort of 'concentrate' them in one big camp."

"Dad and Uncle Jakob *aren't* troublemakers!" I shouted.

"Shush, child." Mama put her finger to her lips. "It'll pass and the Nazis will pick on someone else tomorrow."

I was growing up fast. Though I was fairly small and skinny, my mind was filling out faster than my body – what with all the changes going on around me. Like many Jews, I learned to live with the taunts and stupidities; we just had to cope as best we could.

It was my birthday on the twenty-first of November. Birthdays are birthdays. Nothing was going to spoil it. As usual, Mama baked a cake, sticking eleven little pink candles into the white icing. She drew a picture of a little princess in pink icing on the top.

I'd invited six school friends – beside Hans and Erich. My best friend Suse's mother promised to bring Suse and pick up the others along the way, since it would be growing dark by the time the party got underway.

I was so excited. Mama had given me a little ballerina doll as a birthday present. It had a blue taffeta tutu, white satin shoes and a pink bodice; its blonde hair was tied in a bun and it had bright rosy cheeks. I sat her on the chair next to me as I waited for the guests to arrive.

Four o'clock came.

"They'll be here any moment," called Mama from the kitchen.

Hans arrived with Erich from their Aliyah Jewish club. Both wished me Happy Birthday and gave me presents. I put them on a little table in the corner, still in their wrapping paper, to set beside the other gifts from my friends. Then, after the party, I could open them all together.

Four thirty. "They should have been here by now," said Mama, bustling about impatiently. At five o'clock Mama rang Suse's mother. Suse's father answered. All I could hear were Mama's shocked reactions. "But why? *You* of all people! Working with the Nazis? But Hannah and Suse are best friends. Oh, I see... what does Suse say? Wait, I'll call Hannah..."

Putting her hand over the receiver, Mama

beckoned me over, whispering, "They're not coming." I couldn't believe it.

"Hello, Suse. What's happened?" I was talking to my best friend. Yet it didn't sound like her at all.

"Father says I mustn't talk to you any more."

"But why?"

"He says he could lose his job if the Nazis knew his daughter was friends with a Jew."

"Oh."

"Bye."

I put the phone down slowly, unable to believe my ears. Suse of all people! Her father had been a good friend of Papa's for years. *We'd* been best of friends. I stared at the birthday cake and the little rosy-cheeked ballerina. Taking her in my arms, I rocked her gently and told her not to cry.

Suse hadn't even wished me Happy Birthday. She wasn't the only one. Gradually, our non-Jewish friends began to avoid us, crossing the road whenever they saw us coming. What was even worse, some now looked at us with hate-filled eyes, as if we were to blame. As if we had somehow deceived or betrayed them.

A few days after my birthday disappointment, our loyal maid, Helga, came to the door in her hat and coat. Instead of letting herself in with the spare key, she rang the bell.

Mama answered the door and, thinking Helga must have mislaid her key, invited her in.

"Come and have a glass of tea," Mama said. Helga stood there, looking confused, unable to cross the threshold.

"No, thank you, Frau Kanel. I can't stay."

"What's the matter, Helga? Your husband poorly again?"

"Uh, no." Mama sensed something was wrong. Helga had tears in her eyes and was fidgeting with our key in her fingers.

"I've come to return the key," she said quietly.

"I see," murmured Mama. "I suppose you won't be needing it any more."

Helga looked as if she wanted the floor to swallow her up. "It's not me, Frau Kanel... You see..."

She was having trouble getting the words out. Her face was so miserable, I stood up from the table and went to take her hand. A teardrop fell on my wrist. With an effort, she forced out the words we knew were coming.

"My husband, you know, what with his being in the Party and that... he says I shouldn't come here any more. You know, because you're... well, you know, Jews. It might get him into trouble."

She patted me fondly on the head, as if that helped

to soften the blow, "I'm sorry."

Before we could say anything she thrust the key into my hand and ran off sobbing. I stood, watching her blue hat spiralling down the staircase.

Helga – one of the family.

Helga – who'd been with us for over ten years.

Helga – who'd nursed me through mumps and measles.

Sadly, I rubbed her teardrop into my skin so that it would stay with me forever.

Chapter Four

Bit by bit, life got back to normal. Back to 'Nazi normal', that is.

At least I was spared more 'sticks and stones' at school by a new law banning Jews from German schools. The only trouble was that Hans and I had to walk three kilometres to the Jewish school, which was staffed entirely by Jewish teachers fired from state schools.

All we talked about, day and night, was *how to get out of Germany*. How were we to escape to somewhere safe? German borders were sealed. Nobody wanted us. It was obvious the Nazis were doing all they could to make life impossible. If they couldn't kick us out, however, what else were they planning to do?

Not only were we now driven out of German schools, a new law barred Jews from owning property or business. And Jewish families had to hand over their jewellery.

News of Papa finally came in early December. It was on a printed card from somewhere called Buchenwald, and signed 'FK' at the bottom. He asked for stout boots and warm underclothes.

That same day, a similar card arrived at Jakob Levy's address. But with a difference. The card asked for a ransom for safe passage home from the camp.

"Why no ransom for Friedrich?" Mama asked her sister when they compared cards.

"Maybe only shopkeepers have to pay?" offered Aunt Rachel.

"Sounds odd to me."

Her suspicions grew when she asked around; all her friends had to pay a ransom if they wanted their menfolk back. So why wasn't Papa worth a ransom? Had something happened?

The answer wasn't long in coming. In late December we received a postcard. As I fetched it from the postbox along with the daily paper, the large printed words caught my eye:

YOUR HUSBAND DIED OF
A HEART ATTACK.

No signature. No address. No details. I caught my breath and stifled a scream, "Oh no! Papa's dead!"

Mama came running, snatching the card from my hands. "I don't believe it!" she cried, staring at the card. "He was as strong as an ox. They murdered him, I know it!"

She seemed to have used up all her tears because the tragic news produced no wailing or sobbing, not even a squeezed-out teardrop. Her teeth were clenched tight as she forced out every word, "Children, we are on our own. Your father is dead."

Mama proved to be right. Two days later, Uncle Jakob was released. He lost no time in coming round with news. "Friedrich protested at the guards taking away our braces and shoelaces. You know what he's like. So they beat him to death in front of us."

Uncle Jakob's blunt words produced tearful screams; we wept on each other's shoulders. We cried and cried and didn't want to stop. Mama said to Hans and me, "Children, remember this, your father died because he was a strong, proud man who stood up for others."

I will never forget those words.

We'd heard a German broadcast from the BBC – though we weren't supposed to tune in to foreign stations. The announcer was saying how at last people were waking up to the true nature of the Nazi regime. Crystal Night had finally convinced them. What the British couldn't understand was why a nation that prided itself on good order could go in for such wanton destruction of property and business.

As a response, Jews in England were setting up a relief organisation for German-Jewish refugees. This organisation was to help get them out, guaranteeing foster homes for children and jobs and money for young people to start a new life. At first the British government refused to take in *any* refugees, but then it relented and agreed to take in only children under sixteen. They would come on the *Kindertransport*, Children's Transport, by train from Germany to Holland, and then by ship to England. This news gave us hope.

One day, Mama came in, waving papers over her head. We were so excited. She'd brought our passports with their now-familiar red 'J' for Jew (this 'J' was now our pass to a new life), a visa for England and one-way tickets for the train and boat trip.

Seeing all the papers for the first time produced mixed feelings. I was very excited about going to England with my brother, yet I was sad at leaving Mama and all the other grown-ups.

"Don't worry," said Mama with a smile. "It won't be for long. I have to stay behind to settle Papa's affairs. Then I'll join you over there. It won't be long. You'll see."

Deep down, I felt that her words about staying 'to settle Papa's affairs' were just to stop us worrying. But none of us could speak our fears out loud.

We were due to depart on 30th March 1939, at six thirty in the morning, from Hamburg's Central Station.

Mama woke us around five in the morning. It

was still dark outside and we talked in whispers so as not to wake the others. Everything we were taking was waiting in the hallway. Especially for the journey we had brand new overcoats of thick tweed with velvet collars. Mama had bought them cheaply from W. Israel's clothing shop, after it had been closed down.

"Everyone wears them in England," Mr Israel had said. "Just like Sherlock Holmes."

"I hope I don't have to smoke a pipe then," Hans joked.

Each of us was allowed a small suitcase for spare clothes and other bits and pieces. Hans had Papa's old toilet bag from the Great War, with soap, toothbrush, toothpaste and flannel for the pair of us. In our pockets we had money to last the journey – just ten Reichsmarks; that was the limit.

As going-away presents, I had a new fountain pen, and Hans had a precious birthday gift – Papa's practice violin.

"You'll need money in England," said Mama. "And since you aren't permitted to take any jewellery out, the violin will come in handy. It should fetch quite a lot of money."

Besides the suitcase with my name on a luggage label, I had a shoulder bag containing an apple and sandwich, as well as one other item: the ballerina doll Mama'd given me for my birthday. Though I was really too big for dolls, she gave me a lot of comfort. I called her Miss Hope.

It started to rain as we slipped out, a cold thin drizzle that matched our mood. We were thankful for the tweed overcoats. On his head Hans wore a Sherlock Holmes deerstalker cap, while I had on a stripy brown woollen hood.

It was a good forty-minute walk to the station and, apart from one or two stragglers, the rain-spattered streets were deserted. At the station, though, were crowds of children and grown-ups. The train was due to leave at six thirty and no one really knew what to expect. Would we have seats or not? Would we have to stand in open wagons? Would there be enough room for everyone?

First Mama took us to the 'collection point' to be ticked off a long list and issued with labels to tie round our necks. My label had the number two hundred and fifty-two on it. Hans's was two hundred and fifty-one.

"There," joked Mama, "all you need is a stamp and we can send you through the post to England."

"Where now?" she asked the woman sitting at the trestle table.

"Best grab a seat on the train, if you can," replied the woman. "It's packed. Next!"

Mama forced her way along the platform. It was just as well we'd arrived early – there were still seats to be had. Pulling open a carriage door near the back of the train, she pushed us inside.

"These seats free?" she asked a pale-faced boy in the far corner. He stared at her, a scared look on his face, as if he expected her to take his seat and kick him off the train. Mama ignored him. "Right, sit down, children, while I put your cases on the luggage rack."

Hans sat in one window seat; I flopped down opposite, tired after the long walk and having to carry my heavy suitcase. Feeling sorry for the young boy, I smiled reassuringly to make him feel at ease.

"Where's your mother?" I asked.

He didn't reply. But tears started in his eyes and he looked down at his hands.

"Let him be," whispered Mama.

She busied herself with little chores – brushing the rain from our hats, checking over the sandwiches, opening the violin case to take a last look at Papa's old violin. All the while, she was asking questions she'd already asked a dozen times.

"What time is it?... What time do you arrive at the

Dutch border?… Are you warm enough?… Do you have your visas, tickets and passports?"

Then Mama gave us some last-minute instructions and a promise. "The English like politeness. Always say 'please' and 'thank you'. Each morning, when you get up, say 'Hello, how are you today?' Clean your teeth and comb your hair once the train starts; the toilet's down the corridor. Don't gobble your food all at once; it has to last you until Amsterdam. Write as soon as you can. I'll write every day, let you know when I'm coming…"

Fortunately for us all, the train suddenly hooted like an old man giving his nose a good blow, and a metallic voice came over the loudspeaker, "Attention! The train for Amsterdam is about to leave. The train for Amsterdam is about to leave."

Mama quickly kissed us on both cheeks, and stepped down on to the platform, winding down the window. By now, the carriage was full, with eight children; adults were crowding round the window, waving a last farewell.

As the train heaved and sighed on its way, we could see Mama running along the platform, tears streaming down her face. She'd held back until the very last moment. "I'll… be… coming… s-s-oo-n… " drifted to us on a rush of smoky air.

I was so sad to be leaving Mama behind. Yet I felt excited at the train journey, the boat trip, a new land, a new home, safety. I didn't cry; I took out Miss Hope from my shoulder bag and showed her the houses and cobblestone streets flashing by the open window.

Hans quickly pushed up the window to shut out the drizzle and cold air. He was silent, just gazing out at nothing in particular.

The little boy in the corner was sobbing as if his heart would break. The older children around him were doing their best to cheer him up, offering sweets and apples. But nothing would console him. Luckily, the rocking of the train eventually lulled him to sleep, and his dark curly head fell on the shoulder of the girl next to him.

Even then, his little chest heaved and broken sighs would slip out now and then. Poor lad. I couldn't help wondering what had happened to his family and why no one had seen him off.

In contrast, two of the boys opposite were laughing and playing a game of 'I Spy'. An older girl, about fourteen, joined in. Hans and I kept to ourselves, thinking our own thoughts. It wasn't long before my eyes began to close and I dozed off, waking up with a start every time we stopped at a station.

At one station, dozens of black-uniformed

policemen boarded the train. Mama had warned us we'd be searched and checked. She'd also told us to be extra polite, not to give them an opportunity to send us back.

"And make sure no one's concealing anything unlawful!" she'd said sternly. "If just one person is caught smuggling money or jewellery, the whole lot of you will be sent back, and never let out again."

As we sat quietly waiting for the police, we hoped no one in our carriage would get us into trouble.

Chapter Five

Two figures in Nazi uniform, one tall, one short, flung open the door. "Passports!" the short one shouted as the other pointed to our suitcases on the rack.

While the short one checked the eight passports, the tall one made us open our cases and then searched our belongings. He seemed disappointed until his hand emerged from one case, holding a stamp album. "Aha! What's this?" he hissed.

"That's mine," said one of the 'I Spy' boys. "I collect stamps."

"Not allowed," said the officer. "What's your name?"

"Jacobus," said the boy.

The lanky policeman stepped forward and slapped the boy across the face. "There's another stamp for your collection! Say 'sir' when you address me!"

"Yes, sir. Jacobus, sir."

While the search was going on, his colleague, who bore the SS insignia, seemed to have found something of interest in Hans's passport. "Hmmm," he mused. "Twenty-ninth of March 1923. Your date of birth?"

"Yes, sir," replied Hans nervously.

"So, you're sixteen?"

"Yes, sir."

"Do you know the age limit for this train?"

"Uh, yes, sir."

"What is it?"

"Sixteen, sir."

"Oh no, it isn't! It's *under* sixteen. You are a day over."

Hans looked confused. "But... when they issued my visa I was under," he mumbled.

"And now you're *over*, aren't you?"

"Yes, sir."

The two men both looked at Hans with a grim smile on their lips.

"Come with me," said the short man.

Dumbly Hans followed him out of the carriage.

It surely wouldn't take long to sort out the muddle? They couldn't send him back now! He had his ticket. His case was on the rack, the violin... No, no! He couldn't be sent back now!

After ten minutes the train slowly chugged out of the station. Hans hadn't returned. Nor did I catch a glimpse of him through the train window.

Soon after the train had left, one of the older boys suddenly let out a yell, "Look! We're in No-Man's Land!"

He sprang up and pushed down the window. Leaning out as far as he could, he shouted at the passing fields, "We're free! We're free!"

It was impossible to take in: everything looked the same. The fields were just as muddy brown, the cows were black and white, the sky was cloudy grey, and yellow buttercups and primroses dotted the green banks.

"Are we out of Germany?" asked a girl who'd been asleep.

"Yes, yes, yes."

Everyone except me leapt up, hugged each other and waved whatever they had – hankies, scarves, scraps of paper – out of the window. For the first time, the little boy in the corner had a smile on his face. At the back of our cheering group he was on his feet, waving his little fists in the air. I was too concerned with thoughts of Hans, but quietly I showed Miss Hope the cows and sheep chewing the grass, as if they hadn't a care in the world.

"See, Hope," I told her. "We're free. See how contented the cows look."

All at once, our happy party went deathly quiet. The door flew open and police entered. Immediately we took our seats and sat stock still, arms folded as in school. But these were different police, in light green uniforms. And... they were smiling.

"Good morning, boys and girls," an officer said in a strange accent. "Welcome to Holland. May we see your papers please?"

At first I thought it was a trick. After knowing only bullies and thugs in uniform for six years, I couldn't help but distrust them. I saw from the scared faces of my companions they felt the same.

"Come on, we won't bite you," said the second officer. "You're safe now – as long as your papers are in order."

Their friendly manner encouraged me to ask a question. "Have you seen my brother, Hans Kanel? The Nazis took him away."

"Why's that?" asked one.

"They said he was sixteen. But he's only one day over."

The man shook his head.

"No, miss, sorry. I'll make enquiries."

"Thank you, sir."

When the Dutchmen had gone, my travelling companions did their best to comfort me.

"He'll be all right, you'll see, probably waiting for you at the docks."

"Don't worry, Hannah. You know how the Nazis love order. As soon as they've put your brother's papers in order, he'll follow on."

My concerns for Hans broke the ice. Even the little boy told us his name, Majloch.

"But people call me Max," he said with a shy smile.

It turned out his family – mother, father and elder brothers – were all dead, beaten up and murdered in their grocery shop on Crystal Night.

Although nobody's story was as tragic as Max's, everyone's family had suffered, losing business, home and their living. Apart from Max, we pledged to do all we could to help our relatives escape.

After another couple of hours, the train pulled into Amsterdam where we changed trains. This second train took us right into the docks. And there, gently swaying, was a big black ship with the word *BOTEGRATAN* in white letters on its bows.

We cast off late at night. Once the ship started heaving and groaning through the waves, Max's happy mood changed and he lay still on his bunk, afraid of the creaking, shuddering and rolling; he was certain we were going to sink.

Early next morning, the ship gave a final shudder before bumping into something. I guessed we'd docked in England, at the port called Harwich. My heart leapt. Somehow I felt safer on an island, with Hitler on the other side of the sea.

I could see a streaky pale dawn through the porthole, the round cheesy moon reluctant to depart the sky.

I struggled with the two suitcases, mine and Hans's,

while Max carried the violin case. We followed the crowd off the ship, down the gangplank and into the immigration shed.

Nearly everyone's bag was being searched and children were having to turn out their pockets. When it came to us, the officer looked hard at Max and me, asking suspiciously, "Anything to declare?"

I answered for both of us, since Max spoke no English, remembering Mama's warning always to be polite in England.

"No, sir."

"Any gold? Earrings, necklaces, rings?"

"No, sir."

"What's this then?" He pointed to the violin case. "Let's take a look."

He took the case from under Max's arm and clicked it open.

"Aha!" he said knowingly. "This'll fetch a pretty penny. What's it worth?"

My English wasn't good enough to explain about my brother, so I made the sign of putting a violin under my chin and drawing a bow across it.

"Oh, so you *actually* play, do you? A regular young Paganini!"

I could see he didn't believe me. My red face probably gave me away – I always blush when I tell a lie, I'd never make a good spy.

"Perhaps you'd like to give us a tune?" he said sarcastically.

Handing me the violin, he winked to his mate at the next counter. I couldn't play a note! Papa had never taught me. The game was up. Farewell, violin! Sorry, Papa.

Then a miracle happened. Little Max took the violin from me, put it under his chin and started to pluck at the strings to tune it. Then, taking the bow and wiping it on a hanky, he stroked it across the strings.

He played the sweetest music I'd heard since Papa's playing.

Everyone — immigration officers and children from the *Kindertransport* — stopped what they were doing and listened. The Customs Officer standing before us stared in amazement, a dreamy look coming into his eyes.

"Beautiful," he breathed. "Do you know anything else?"

Perhaps he thought Max had practised just one tune to fool them. Putting the instrument back under his chin, Max played what I remembered as an old German tune, *Heil dir im Siegerkrantz*. The moment he started playing, however, the officer did something very odd. He pulled himself up straight and stood to attention until Max had finished. How strange the English are! Only afterwards did I learn that the tune was also the British national anthem, 'God Save the King!' Loud clapping rang out and the Customs Officer smiled broadly, tears in his eyes.

"Play your violin, sonny," he said with a frog in his throat. "I'll come to hear you in the Albert Hall. God bless you. And good luck to you both.

"Right. Next…"

Waiting in the rain was a long row of red buses. How peculiar: they were like houses, with upstairs and downstairs. Beside each one stood an odd figure in shiny boots, dark blue flower pot-helmet and black cape. At first I thought it was an English sailor. The truth didn't enter my head. It was an English policeman!

How could it be? This man had no gun, he was *smiling*, patting children on the head, taking their hands and carrying their bags. "Come on, ducky, give us your cases," he called as he helped Max and me onto the bus.

When the red buses were full, they drove off – past small, odd-coloured houses with little gardens at the front and orange chimneys on slate roofs with smoke curling out of them.

Our bus followed the sea road for about twenty

minutes until we came to what looked like a holiday camp. Only later did we discover it *was* a holiday camp called 'Dovercourt'. Since it was too cold and wet for holidays at this time of year, the buildings were to be a temporary home for refugees, and this is where we stayed.

Chapter Six

It was a long, long time before I was found a 'home'. War broke out between England and Germany, then Hitler started bombing England – so I wasn't so safe on my island, after all.

Max had been fixed up with a musical family, but no one seemed to want a little girl who couldn't play music, cook, darn or milk cows. The wait gave me time to take English lessons; apart from a slight accent, I was eventually able to speak good English. At long last, I was told of a 'possible evacuation place'. But, the matron said, "You'll have to muck in and muck out, get your hands dirty. They need a big, strapping youth to help out on the farm."

"That's me!" I exclaimed. I really wanted to leave Dovercourt. Matron peered over her glasses at me. "You don't look very strapping for someone who's coming up to fourteen. Are you religious?" I thought about that one. *Was* I religious?

"I don't really know," I murmured.

"Mmm. You see, this Mrs Pittaway is most precise. 'No orthodox Jews, no Catholics, no Christadelphians'."

"I'm none of those," I hastened to assure her. She made up her mind. "Well, she's prepared to accept a female who'll work really hard. I'll recommend you."

"Thank you, Matron."

"One more thing. What are we to call you?"

I didn't understand.

"The English like simple, English-sounding names. It helps you fit in, see. The last boy I fixed up, Peter Morgenstern, changed his name to Peter Morgan. What with all this anti-German feeling about, it's for the best."

"What do you suggest?" I asked. "I wouldn't want to lose Hannah."

"Hannah's fine. Let me see... Kanel? Canal? Camel? Canning? Ye-ess, Canning sounds better. I'll write it in brackets after Kanel. You don't have to use it if you don't want to."

A few days later, she summoned me to her office for new instructions. "You are to be on the ten twenty-four train from Waterloo to Portsmouth Harbour on the morning of fifteenth September. Mrs Pittaway will be waiting for you at Havant Station. Have you enough money for the fare?"

"I think so," I said, counting the sixpences and shillings in my purse. "I do a bit of washing and ironing for a laundry, and they've been paying me for my work."

"Good. I wish you well, Hannah."

A completely new life was about to open up for me – as a milkmaid. If only Mama could see me, sitting on a milking stool and squeezing cow udders, what would she say?

On my train ride through London, everywhere I looked, to right and left, were piles of broken bricks that had recently been homes and schools. *Germans* had done this, *my* people, *my* country. Perhaps men I'd known. My teachers. The thugs who'd smashed up our flat…

Thoughts of home brought me back to Mama. Eight years of Hitler! From the newspapers I knew that every passing year, month, week, day brought fresh attacks on the Jews. I pictured Mama walking furtively down the street wearing her yellow Star of David – with *real* Germans calling her a 'filthy Jew-pig'. *I had to do something!* But what? War now made escape from Germany impossible.

I fell asleep, dreaming of happier days. Each time the train ground to a halt – at Woking, Guildford, Haslemere, Liphook, Petersfield – passengers came and went, disturbing my dreams of home. But when a voice shouted, 'Next stop Havant!', I took down my case from the rack and stared out at the passing countryside. How sleepy and peaceful it looked by contrast with London!

As the train pulled into Havant Station, I waited, hand on the door handle, ready to jump out. The luggage label on my overcoat said 'Hannah Canning' in thick black letters.

At the barrier, the inspector took my ticket and, looking at my label, jerked a thumb towards a tall, youngish woman in a brown tweed outfit and brown beret. Going up to her, I asked politely, "Mrs Pittaway? Mrs Grace Pittaway?"

"Yes. You're Hannah, I see," she replied, extending a gloved hand.

I shook hands and followed her through the station lobby into the early autumn sunshine. She walked quickly with long strides towards a dusty old farm car where a grizzled man was waiting. At the side door she turned and stared hard at me. From her sour look, she obviously didn't like what she saw.

"You're not Christadelphian, are you?" she said.

"Uh, no," I replied, wondering what a Christadelphian was.

"You don't *look* very Jewish," was her next remark, after looking me up and down. How were Jews supposed to look?

"My real name's Kanel," I offered.

"Come on, me dear," said the old driver. "Best be getting on."

He winked to me as Mrs Pittaway took her seat, leading me round the back of the farm car.

"Jump in, my luvver. It's a tidy old drive."

"Thank you, sir," I said, following my case onto the straw-strewn floor.

We drove along in silence, bumping up and down on country lanes. At one point we came to an abrupt halt to let a herd of cows meander slowly across the road. I don't know why, but I somehow expected them to look different from German cows. From the sly look they gave me, perhaps they thought the same of me. They certainly smelled and mooed the same.

We passed road signs before pretty little villages: Westbourne, Southbourne, Nutbourne; then, all at once, we turned down a rutted path and stopped.

The first sound that greeted me was the loud barking of a dog, accompanied by a chorus of clucking and a shrill 'cock-a-doodle-do' from the backyard.

Almost as soon as I'd scrambled down from the farm car with my case, it drove off again. Mrs Pittaway and I stood facing each other.

Chapter Seven

"Round the back," said my new guardian, striding off down one side of the old whitewashed house. As she unlocked the back door, she threw out another order, "Wipe your feet." I scuffed my boots on a metal grille outside the door and stood, waiting for further orders.

"Come in! Come in, gal! Put down your case. Take off your hat and coat. Sit you down."

I obeyed instructions, taking a seat at the bare wooden table. Over by the sink was a large churn in which Mrs Pittaway now dipped a metal ladle, filling two enamel mugs with creamy milk.

"There, drink up. God's work is waiting."

"Thank you, ma'am," I said, remembering Mama's warning about being polite.

"Don't thank me. Thank God," she said with a sniff.

The English were certainly frosty. Several refugees had warned me of that, though they were supposed to thaw out once you got to know them. Perhaps it was up to me to break the ice.

"I'm sorry about your husband." (Matron had said he'd been shot down over France.)

She darted a sharp glance at me, her eyes showing anger and fear. Then her features softened slightly.

"Thank you," she said quietly.

At once, she threw up her arms, as if casting off a burden, and said with a sigh, "What's done's done. God's will. Life must go on."

I was bursting to ask *my* question. Was this the right time? She gave me an opening by asking, "And your family? I've been told you lost your father."

"Killed by the Nazis," I said. "No news of Mama. Uh, Mrs Pittaway, may I send a postcard home, with an address?"

"Address!" she exclaimed. "What, *this* address?" She seemed confused. "What if the Germans see it, come and drop bombs on me?"

I didn't know what to say. Yet to my surprise she gave a bitter smile. "Let them dare! Of course, write to your mother, tell her to write here. Grace Pittaway is not afraid of Germans."

"Thank you, ma'am." I breathed a sigh of relief.

"Come on, gal! Time and tide wait for no man."

I worked harder than I'd ever done before. Up with the lark, scrubbing the flagstones of kitchen and larder, mucking out the cowshed, feeding chickens and ducks, collecting eggs, milking the cows, rolling the milk churns to the gate at the end of the orchard, where they were collected twice a day. I scarcely had time to breathe.

I was grateful when Sunday came round and we

had to dress up for church. Even though we walked a mile there and back, it was a relief to get away from working my fingers to the bone.

Mrs Pittaway made it clear she'd chosen me, a Jew, to save 'my Jewish soul' and convert me into a good Christian. So she took it upon herself to read the Gospels to me every evening before going to bed and to make sure I said my prayers and grace at every meal.

There were compensations. I could write home as often as I liked. I had a little bedroom all to myself. I ate fresh plums, apples and pears from the orchard, fresh eggs and meat, and I drank as much milk as I liked – even though it was rationed in the towns. So I never went hungry.

My guardian sent me to the local school where I made friends with other children. True, it meant a long walk (the school was a church hall at the back of the local church), but since I had to gather rabbit food on my way home it saved extra foraging in the woods and fields.

Country life soon brought colour to my cheeks and helped build me up. I enjoyed looking after the animals, walking by myself in the woods and especially going to school. No longer was I afraid of Nazi thugs, bombs and death; they were all in the past. But… I constantly worried about Mama and Hans. I'd heard nothing from them since war had broken out.

Not only that, I also missed my old friends, even those who'd deserted me. Nobody here understood me. How could they? I could tell from the look in their eyes they were suspicious. *Is she a German spy?* they were all thinking.

Sometimes I'd pass kids in the playground and they'd suddenly stop talking as if I might overhear secrets: 'Careless Talk Costs Lives' – as the posters warned. Even Mrs Pittaway avoided the subject of war, almost as if I was somehow involved in her husband's death.

Chapter Eight

Unexpectedly, Mrs Pittaway made an announcement, "I'm taking in a couple of evacuees."

We were sitting astride neighbouring milk stools at the time, and her words were accompanied by the *swish-swish* of milk from udder to pail. I wasn't certain what an 'evacuee' was, so I asked.

"Evacuees? Kids from city slums. In these godless times it is my Christian duty."

I was excited by the news. On the farm I missed having other children to play and joke with. And there was the thought of extra hands to share the chores. I was able to gather little more except that their names were Frank and Violet Carter. Frank was a year younger than me, at thirteen, and Violet was eleven. They were from the East End of London. I couldn't wait for their arrival.

Mrs Pittaway was a woman of few words. So I wasn't surprised when, one Saturday lunchtime, she left me in charge without a word of explanation. She wore no make-up, but she did pin her wiry hair back with Kirby grips. Pilot Officer Pittaway's death had plunged her into work and prayer, with no time for 'frivolity'. She was now wedded to God and God's creatures – cows, sheep, chickens and, last of all, lost souls like me who might yet be saved. No doubt our new arrivals, Frank and Violet, were seen as lambs joining the Lord's flock.

We'd been expecting the London evacuees for several days. I'd swept out the attic and made up two bunk beds, shaking creepy-crawlies out of the straw mattresses and airing damp sheets and blankets in front of the kitchen fire. There were no pillowcases, so they, like me, would have to lay their weary heads on stripy, grey, straw-filled bolsters.

I was out collecting logs when Mrs Pittaway returned from her trip. I heard her return to her farm chores and I took the logs indoors. When I backed into the kitchen, I got a shock. A sudden noise at my back frightened the living daylights out of me. Even though I'd been in England for some time, memories of Nazis beating up Jews were always just below the surface. For a split second I expected to see an officer in a black SS uniform pointing a gun at my head and asking where my yellow star was.

The evacuees from London! Poor souls, they were sitting at the table in their hats and coats, with luggage labels still pinned to their collars. Round their necks were pieces of white string holding gas masks.

How odd! Didn't they know we didn't need gas masks in the country? I immediately felt sorry for them, obviously tired out from the long trek from the railway station, snatched away from their mama and papa. The little girl looked on the verge of tears. She sat, hands in her lap, watery blue eyes giving colour to her pasty face. Her thin mauve lips were pressed tight, as if trying to keep in the sobs.

As for the boy, he was the opposite, looking down his nose at me as if I was the housemaid, with a superior grin on his freckled face. Was he one of those boys who treated all girls as stupid?

What further put me against him were the tufts of carroty hair poking out from under a school cap and his snotty nose which he kept wiping with the back of his hand. He stood up and introduced them both in a loud voice. Despite his dirty hand, I shook hands with him and his sister, saying, "I'm Hannah. Hannah Kanel."

I deliberately used my proper, *German*, name. Clearly, Mrs Pittaway hadn't said who I was, for the little girl frowned at my accent and wanted to know if I was a 'foreigner'. When I told them I was German I could see a hostile look come into the boy's eyes. His sister's blue eyes, however, shone with excitement.

I didn't mind. Perhaps I was the same at her age, a bit curious. I knew she didn't mean to be rude. But I could see the boy didn't like me.

After showing them their attic bedroom and answering a few more questions, I was glad to get back to my chores – the animals asked no questions and didn't object to German hands patting their hides or squeezing their udders.

What really made me nervous about the newcomers was that they'd annoyed Mrs Pittaway. I didn't know exactly what it was they had done, but as I sat next to her in the dairy, making butter, I could see her shoulders twitching as shouts and hoots reached us from the house and farmyard. That was followed by silly mooing and eeh-awh-ing noises.

On top of it all someone woke up Rufus, and he started barking, kicking up an awful row and putting the animals on edge. Frank and Violet must have brought their war games from London, because we could hear the boy rushing about yelling and the hens clucking in alarm.

Finally, Mrs Pittaway had had enough. When she spotted the boy's ginger head peering round the dairy door, she gave him and his sister a piece of her mind.

"Hey, you! This here's a farm, not the London slums! You're upsetting my animals and scaring my layers. Make yourselves useful. Go and collect them eggs!"

If she thought that would put an end to their high spirits she was mistaken. They obviously had no idea where to look! They didn't even seem to know what it was that laid them! When I went out and showed them the chicken coop, they stared at me as if I'd pointed to a snake pit...

Not long after, they set off Rufus again. This time it sounded like he was tearing one of them to pieces, biting great chunks out of them. From the cowshed we could hear wailing, thumping and shouting, "Get orff!"

As I rushed out again, I stopped in my tracks. There before me was the funniest sight anyone could imagine.

The boy, Frank, was sprawling in the muck heap, his head covered in cow dung and wet straw, one of his shoes in Rufus's teeth and a wet patch over the front of his shorts, as if he'd weed himself. Egg yolk was running down his legs. I could hardly stop myself from laughing.

Naturally, Mrs Pittaway didn't see the funny side. The smashed eggs were the last straw. When she realized what had happened, she went raving mad, swearing she'd send the hooligans back to London.

"My eggs! My eggs!" she kept shrieking.

The trouble was that 'her' eggs were collected from the farm every day and sent to feed the towns. Now she wouldn't be able to meet her quota.

"Folk'll go hungry because of you!" she screamed. "Eggs is precious. They help win the war. They're ammunition against the Devil's hordes! You're nothing but... but... *saboteurs.*"

Having found the foulest word in her vocabulary, she repeated it over and over, "Saboteurs! Saboteurs! Saboteurs!" That was followed by, "You should be shot!"

Frank and Violet were sent to bed without any supper. I think they were glad to escape their host's fury. Maybe they were plotting to run away to London. I couldn't say I blamed them. What a first day on the farm!

But thoughts of sympathy disappeared thanks to Mrs Pittaway, who now turned on me. "It's all your fault! You should never have let them out of your sight! I can't be everywhere, can I?"

Chapter Nine

The farther away from war I was and the more peaceful my nights were, strangely enough the worse I felt. Although I'd slept soundly in the Dovercourt chalets, I now began to have nightmares and wake up sweating and crying.

One dream kept coming over and over again. I was in a big prison camp surrounded by barbed wire. Just women and girls wearing grey prison smocks. We were being made to jump over a wooden fence... on the other side of which was a big hole full of squirming bodies. I woke up, screaming, just as I leapt into the pit...

That wasn't the only fear my imagination conjured up. In the evening, before going to bed, I'd stare into the dying embers of the fire and see terrifying sights: Mama being bundled into a truck and taken away somewhere; Hans wasting away to a skeleton for want of food. And there, over in the corner, under that smouldering log, Uncle Jakob's family was hiding – a bright torchlight was searching for their hiding place. Then, *crash!* The log burst apart, scattering sparks like bullets.

The scenes were so vivid, they haunted me for days afterwards. I had no one to share my worries with –

apart from my school teacher, Miss Hopkinson. Mrs Pittaway didn't want reminding of her husband's death. Violet was too young to understand. As for Frank, he'd probably laugh in my face, either in disbelief or lack of sympathy for foreigners, especially Germans. Would he know the difference between a German and a German-Jew?

Only the cows were sympathetic. I knew they listened to me because they twitched their ears and nodded, now and again mooing softly, as if to say: "We understand, little Hannah."

"I wonder if you do understand?" I asked Betsy as I squeezed her warm milk into the pail. She swished her tail contentedly and nodded, encouraging me to open my heart to her.

I recounted all that had happened: the terrible shock of Crystal Night; the tramping of boots; the knocking at the door; the wardrobe falling on me; the twisted, hate-filled faces of the brown shirts; the smashing of Mama's Meissen dinner set. Worst of all was Papa's look of horror when that lout broke his priceless violin.

Then I told Betsy about the 'circus' show at the old cinema: "You wouldn't believe what those monsters did. They forced old men to strip to their underwear and jump over a chair! What heartless, inhuman beasts! How they laughed when Uncle Jakob fell on his face.

"But not my papa! Oh no. He refused to cringe like a dog. I felt really scared for him, yet, at the same time, very proud. One man was standing up to the thugs – my papa! How they hated him for spoiling their shows. They whipped him. They punched him. But he stood straight and tall, blood streaming down his face. Only when he could bear it no longer did he fall to the floor. But he hadn't given in. Oh, Papa Papa, Papa!"

I couldn't go on. Putting my head against Betsy's warm side, I broke down sobbing my heart out. All at once afraid of someone seeing me, I looked round. I thought I heard footsteps running across the yard. Quickly, I stopped snivelling and wiped my eyes with my wet hands.

That was Betsy done. With a last thank you 'moo', she ambled off, grateful for me confiding in her.

I was reading a book in the library one evening, when Frank thrust what he called his 'find' under my nose. He wouldn't admit to where he'd found it, but the charred German booklet was still warm and smelt of smoke. Violet didn't have his self-control though. "We found it in the long grass near the crashed plane."

I'd heard at school of an enemy plane coming

down in a nearby turnip field. Now, as I held it in my hands, I experienced a strange sensation.

The little book was mine, yet not mine, my language, yet nothing I would ever say. But I could see Frank and Violet couldn't understand that.

With Frank standing over me, I had no choice but to translate the title and a few sentences. The words 'Kill the Jews!' struck terror into my heart. Yet to my astonishment, Frank at first thought I was making them up.

I think he got a shock when I told him I was a Jew. Not that he or Violet really knew what a Jew was. He made me so furious I stamped off to bed. You can't reason with the unreasonable.

As Mrs Pittaway didn't hold with wireless or newspapers, I had only Miss Hopkinson at school who kept the class informed of battles and events in Germany. She also asked me about my family. I told her about Mama, Hans, Uncle Jakob, Aunt Rachel and Erich. She had a troubled look in her hazel eyes as she listened. "Hannah," she said quietly. "I think things will get worse before they get better. Let's hope and pray your family will see it through."

I tried to press her further. What had she heard? She said she was reluctant 'to worry me unnecessarily'.

Chapter Ten

I was in the middle of mucking out the cowshed next day, when I heard someone urgently shouting, "Hannah! Hannah!" It was Vi. I was about to tell her off for disturbing Buttercup, who was pregnant and jumped at the slightest upset. But I could tell something was wrong.

Vi came running into the cowshed, all red-faced and out of breath. For one awful moment I thought the Nazis had invaded and were coming to take me away.

"Come quickly, Han!" she panted.

"I can't go anywhere until I've finished mucking out," I told her.

Her next words brought about my worst fears. "We've caught a German!"

She was so excited, she spoke as if she'd just caught her first fish in the stream. Of course, I didn't believe her – not *caught* a German. You don't *catch* Germans. You might see one in an aeroplane. She was lucky Mrs Pittaway was at Emsworth market or she'd have ordered Vi to wash her mouth out with soap and water for telling fibs.

"Oh, Han, you *must* come," she pleaded. "He could die. He's badly wounded. We need you to talk to him. Come on, come, hurry!"

Was it true? Maybe a prisoner-of-war had escaped from one of the camps at Fort Purbrook or Fort Widley on Portsdown Hill.

"Calm down, Violet," I said as firmly as I could. "Take a deep breath. Count to ten. That's it. Slo-o-wly."

While she was counting, I asked two questions, "Who is this German? How did he get here?"

Realising I wouldn't go with her unless she explained, she tried once more, this time in answer to my questions, "He fell from the sky, last night, from the crashed plane. We found him in the woods, hanging from his parachute, caught up in the trees. There were two of them, but Frank reckons one's had his chips. But this one's alive, moaning like a ghost. He didn't half give us the frighteners."

"How is he hurt?"

"That's the trouble. We don't know. He's bleeding, he may have broken bones. If *you* speak to him he can tell you what's broken. When I left him his eyes were shut and he was as white as a sheet, as if someone'd uncorked his blood and poured it away."

So it looked like it was true. A German pilot had bailed out! A shiver ran right through me. Vi could see I wasn't keen to go with her. "Oh, please, Hannah. Frank says he's got secrets… to help us win the war."

I thought about it. Well, yes, Frank could be right. Not win the war, exactly, but give an idea of German bombing strength, when and where raids were planned. I suppose I owed it to my adopted country to help.

"All right, Vi," I said, lifting the last batch of wet straw on to the wheelbarrow. "I'm finished here anyway. Show me the way."

Grabbing my scarf from a rusty nail, I followed her through the trees to the north of the railway line. She wasn't too sure where she was going; if it hadn't been for Frank hello-ing back to our echoing shouts we might never have found the clearing. All at once, through the trees, I caught sight of red hair lit up in a slanting shaft of sunbeams.

"Over here," came a half-muffled shout. We pushed a way through bracken and bramble until we reached him.

"About time too!" he muttered ungratefully. "What kept you?"

It was then I saw the body. An airman still hooked up to the parachute that had saved his miserable life. By the coarse breathing I could tell he was still alive. I'd never set eyes on a Nazi in England before. I gazed down with a mixture of fear and loathing. This was the Enemy. A monster who'd smashed up our home.

A cut-throat who slit the throats of little children. I felt more like kicking than helping him.

"Do what you can to keep him alive," ordered Frank. "I'm off to fetch the police."

He left Vi and me alone with the prisoner. Not that the enemy was likely to overpower us in his state. *Not at the moment...*

Although I hated even touching him, I forced myself – in order to try to save his life. If I didn't help him breathe, he'd soon choke to death. That much was obvious. What we needed was water to clean him up.

But what were we to carry it in? Maybe he had a can or some cup in his knapsack? Trouble was, I couldn't bring myself to touch him or his belongings.

"Vi, see if there's a cup or can in his pack," I said. "Something to pour water into." Like me, she was too scared to touch any of his stuff. "Think of the soldiers in the war!" I'd heard Frank say that to her. It worked a treat. With trembling fingers she unfastened the pack from his back and rummaged inside, hardly bearing to look, as if it were full of spiders. All at once, she cried out, "Bingo!"

I didn't know what she meant until she drew out a tin cup.

"That'll do nicely. Well done. Now, here's an easier task: go and fill it with water. There are a good few pools around. Then bring it back quickly!"

As Vi ran off, I swallowed hard. It was now *my* turn to be brave. The pilot needed urgent attention! For some reason, the image of Dad lying in a pool of blood on that cinema stage flashed before me. No one had rushed to his assistance. Those men just stood and mocked him. Part of me wanted revenge, for Papa's sake. But what would Papa have done in my place? Yes, I know…

I pulled out a hanky from my smock pocket and moistened it with my tongue. Holding my breath, I counted to ten, then, with one hand holding up his head, I first rubbed off the caked blood from his nose and mouth. Having undone the helmet strap, I wiped sweat and dirt off his forehead and brushed twigs and leaves from his hair. He had a bad gash behind one ear – as soon as I started to clean it, bright red blood trickled out. How was I to stop the flow? He might bleed to death.

I looked round for an old rag. Nothing but twigs and leaves. There was no alternative: I unbuttoned my smock and tore a strip off the bottom of my one and only vest, using it as a bandage. Winding it round his head, I tied a knot at the opposite side to the wound.

Pleased with my medical skills, I took a good look at him for the first time.

With fair hair tumbling over his brow, he looked, well, sort of calm and peaceful, now that his face was cleaned up. I was surprised how young he seemed – almost a boy, about Hans's age. Funny how I'd always pictured Nazis as ugly brutes, just like those who'd smashed up our flat, herded us into the cinema and burnt down the synagogue. Evil. Vicious. Cruel monsters. Yet this lad looked so harmless.

Immediately I shook my head hard, clearing it of unwanted thoughts. I wasn't looking at an innocent young boy in the school playground. This was a murderer. What was I thinking of!

When Vi returned with a tinful of muddy water I washed off the remaining blood and dirt. "That'll do," I said to no one in particular, turning my attention to a badly twisted arm. "It looks broken just below the elbow."

By now I'd overcome my fear of touching him. I imagined his flesh was cow's udders or rump. As my fingers groped for the break, digging into his limp arm, his face creased with pain. He moaned softly and his eyes flickered open.

"Oh, golly!" gasped Vi, jumping back. "He's come alive! He'll do us in."

But our prisoner was in no state to move, let alone do us harm. His dull grey eyes stared out fearfully from sunken sockets, trying to focus on the figures standing over him. It took him a while to take in the situation.

He was obviously in enemy hands, even if we were children. It was hard for him to focus his eyes. He seemed so tired that at that moment he clearly didn't care what happened to him.

I wasn't sure what to do next. All I thought was: *he mustn't die.* As I was wondering what to do, a gurgle came from his throat, startling Vi and me (I thought for a moment he was about to die). His whole body trembled from top to toe, and he lifted the good hand towards his mouth.

"I think he wants a drink," I told Vi.

As I held up his head, Vi put the tin to his dry lips, spilling most of the water down his chin. The wounded pilot wasn't choosy: he swallowed the water greedily. It seemed to revive him a bit for he forced out a word of thanks, this time with a pained smile.

At that he closed his eyes and sank back. His teeth were chattering and beads of sweat were breaking out on his brow, like raindrops on a window pane. "Can't we get him to somewhere warm?" asked Vi, clearly feeling sorry for him.

I'd been thinking that myself. Not that I had any desire to save his miserable skin. It was his fault for being here. The English hadn't invited him over to bomb them. But I needed to stop him dying or escaping before the police arrived. He was my prisoner. My responsibility. *My* contribution to the war.

Though I didn't mention it to Vi, there was something else, something hard to put into words. If I didn't try to save his life, would I be any better than the Nazis who'd killed Papa?

As I was making up my mind, a chill breeze sprang up, swirling the fallen leaves about and blowing through his damp hair; the first drops of rain were falling from the circle of iron-grey sky above us.

"I'd better try to patch up his arm," I said, taking off my scarf.

I made a makeshift sling out of the old grey scarf and, as gently as possible, I tied it round his neck and forearm. The sharp pain as I lifted the arm roused him once more. By now he evidently understood we were trying to help.

Seeing our prisoner looking helpless made Vi bolder. "OK, Fritz," she said in a firm voice. "You – our prisoner. My brother, Frank – he go for police. You not escape. Understand?" She gave him a hard stare. The young man understood the word 'police', for he nodded wearily.

We suddenly heard shouting and crashing through the trees. Frank had arrived with reinforcements to take our prisoner away.

Chapter Eleven

Frank had apparently handed in the charred German book to our teacher. He obviously didn't believe my version of its contents. On Monday morning, right after prayers, Miss Hopkinson asked me to read it out in English. What? How could she! What if I asked her to translate a 'Kill the English' book?

My refusal seemed to make her realize how painful it was for me. Breaktime gave her a chance to think things over, because she obviously decided it was time to tell the class more about Adolf Hitler and the Nazis.

Although I was surprised at how little they knew, I realized Miss Hopkinson was doing it mainly for my benefit. After a while, being shocked at their lack of knowledge, I was ready to join in.

Miss Hopkinson went on to tell the class about the Jews, about the origins of their first language, Hebrew, about the Bible being written originally in Hebrew – the class was sure it had been written in old-fashioned English. It came as more of a shock when she told them Jesus was a Jew. Now, if I had said that, they wouldn't have believed me. But coming from Miss Hopkinson, it *had* to be true.

Several boys and girls turned to take another look

at me, with new respect in their eyes. Not only was I a kinswoman of Jesus, I was *on their side* in the war, since Adolf Hitler was also fighting against the Jews.

Right at the end of the lesson, Miss Hopkinson went and spoiled it by asking me about my family. I suddenly felt tears starting at the back of my eyes. Be brave, Hannah! Don't break down! Go on, tell them!

But I couldn't. It was too painful. They wouldn't understand.

Luckily for me, the school bell rang. End of lessons! The whole class jumped up, ready to rush off home.

NO! I mustn't let them go without telling them. They *have* to know. Frank has *got* to know! They should *all* know what this war meant for the Jews...

Too late I put my hand up.

Miss Hopkinson didn't notice my raised hand. But the girl who shared my desk, Susie, shouted out, "Hannah's got her hand up, Miss!"

"Sit down, children," came Miss Hopkinson's commanding tones. "Yes, Hannah."

I almost spoiled it by flooding what I wanted to say with bitter tears. But I clenched my fists, screwed up my eyes and cleared my throat.

"I've had no word from my family... for nearly three years..."

The classroom fell silent. After a few moments, the

stillness was broken by the teacher's voice, "Thank you, Hannah. All right, children, you can go home now."

A strange thing happened. Instead of dashing helter-skelter out of the classroom, the children sat silently at their desks. Susie slid closer, putting her arm round me and murmuring, "Never mind, Hannah, we'll be your family."

On the way home Vi was full of beans, as usual, showing off her painting and babbling on about a little poem she'd written. Frank, however, was uncommonly quiet.

At school next morning, Miss Hopkinson surprised the class by saying, "Imagine flying away on a magic carpet to Germany, sitting in a German school. You are all German children. Hannah is the only Jew in the class. Now… how would you feel? Just think about it for a while."

Turning to me, she said, "Hannah, come out to the front and tell the class about your schooldays back home in Germany."

I stood up nervously, walking to the front and standing before the blackboard. I could feel all eyes on me, curious, suspicious.

"I'll try, miss," I said, so quietly she had to ask me to speak up, "So that everyone can hear."

"School was fine," I said hoarsely, clearing my throat. "Well, it was until Herr Hitler came to power. Then it all started to go wrong. The first thing that happened was that I was sent to sit in the corner."

"Why was that, Hannah?" asked Miss Hopkinson. She could see the class didn't understand.

"No one was supposed to share a desk with a Jew, or even speak to me."

From the smirk on some pupils' faces, I could see they didn't believe me.

"Were you a dunce?" asked a boy at the back, to a few giggles.

"No, no, I worked ever so hard – and Mama helped me with German, so that I got top marks. Then, all at once, no matter how hard I – or Mama – tried, I received only low marks. One day, I couldn't help myself, I asked our German teacher, Fraulein Ruhl, why…

"She glared at me. I could see a mixture of hatred and triumph in her eyes. When she spoke, she emphasised each word, more for the class than for me, 'Only a *true*, I repeat *t-r-u-e* German can be good at German.'

"A few girls in my class laughed out loud. But Fraulein Ruhl wasn't finished. She said loudly, 'You got what you deserved. In future, don't dare question my marking... or you'll get another mark – on your Jewish bottom!'

"When I came home and told Mama she was very cross: 'That Hitler!' she fumed. 'The man's Austrian. Not a *true* German at all, so he can't be any good at German either!'"

Some of Miss Hopkinson's class laughed. But the teacher held up her hand. "That's terrible, Hannah. Isn't it, class?"

"Yes, miss," they echoed back, some with feeling.

"Does anyone want to ask Hannah a question?"

There was a hush before a boy with glasses in the front row asked, "How about your school friends? Did they still like you?"

"Well, some tried to please the teacher by turning their backs on me. What was worse was being called names in the playground, like *Juden Stinker*, which means 'dirty Jew', or 'Jew pig'. I wasn't dirty and I didn't smell. So why was I a 'stinker'? I wasn't a pig. I was a little girl, a little German girl who happened to be Jewish – like some happen to be ginger and have freckles." I looked at Frank. He lowered his eyes.

"Mama told me to repeat under my breath, 'Sticks and stones may break my bones, but names will never hurt me.' All the same, it hurt. At playtime, some of the girls wouldn't let me join their skipping or hopscotch.

And one day, a couple of older girls came up and started poking me in the chest, chanting 'Jew girl! Jew girl! Jew girl!'

"To get away from them, I ran off to find my best friend Suse. But they chased me and tripped me up. It had been raining and I fell into a puddle, grazing my knees and tearing my stockings. I knew Mama would be cross with me for getting my skirt and jacket muddy.

"It was too much. I burst into tears, begging them to leave me alone. What had I ever done to them? From then on, I sat in the toilets at lunchtime, eating my sandwiches there, hoping I wouldn't be found.

"But I still had a few friends. My best friend Suse stood by me. Whenever she could she put herself between me and the bullies, giving as good as she got. If it hadn't been for Suse I don't know what I'd have done.

"It was not only schoolchildren, but also teachers who were becoming spiteful. The lesson I came to hate most was Physical Training. A new teacher had taken over and she wanted to develop our bodies and make us fit for hard work so we could be what she called perfect Germans.

"She was a middle-aged woman with short ash-blonde hair. Since I was the only Jew in the class, she devised a special punishment for me. The class was taking turns, jumping over the horse – run-up, hands on horse, leap up, legs follow through, land on the other side. Only one or two of us could do it properly without help. So the teacher stood by the horse to catch us as we vaulted. When it was my turn, however, she suddenly stepped aside, letting me crash to the floor, bumping my nose and grazing my knees. She then had the chance she wanted to call me all sorts of names."

The classroom had gone quiet. Everyone was gazing up at me, clearly wanting to hear more. Perhaps some of them were putting themselves in my shoes, wondering how they would feel if it happened to them.

Pamela in the back row put up her hand and asked, "Were all the teachers nasty?"

"No, some were decent. Some of the older ones were stuck in their ways, strict with everyone, without exception. But some, mostly the younger ones had it in for me. The odd thing was that, before Hitler appeared on the scene, no one regarded me as a Jew at all. I was German, like anyone else."

Pamela was very interested, but puzzled. "If you're German, you must be Aryan. But if you're Jewish you can't be Aryan."

"Yes, I don't understand it either," I said. "One day we were told that all blood's the same. Blood's blood – like blue sky or salty sea. Then Hitler said that *Aryans* have one sort of blood, pure blood, and *non-Aryans* have another, unclean, full of germs. Next thing we knew the Nazis passed a law banning Germans from marrying Jews or Gypsies. Why? Because the children would turn out to be cripples or loonies.

"Lessons were changing. Not just PT. Biology was even worse. It was taken by a small, bald-headed man who used to be so meek and mild. But once he put on a uniform, he became a totally different person.

"He joined the SS, the *Schutz-Staffel*, Hitler's special police force. Each day he would strut, not walk, to school in his black uniform, with knee-high jackboots. As if that weren't enough to scare us, he kept a black revolver in a holster of his right boot. Would you believe, he used to take it out and wave it at the class every time he got excited.

"His favourite topic was 'Aryans and Jews'. At the start of every class, the biology master would ask the same question: 'why are Germans the Master Race?' Without waiting for an answer, he'd say, 'Because we're Aryans.' We had to repeat after him, 'We Germans are the Master Race because we're Aryans.'

I would chant with the rest, even though I had no idea what an Aryan was. Then he would insist we keep our race pure by marrying another Aryan. That made us laugh – we were much too young to be thinking about getting married. Also, there weren't enough so-called Aryan boys to go round. Some of us might have to make do with weedy specimens like the biology teacher – or Adolf Hitler for that matter.

"I dreaded what was coming next: he asked the same question every lesson. 'We must root out alien elements. What are alien elements?' His pet pupil, Gretl, answered every time, 'Jews, sir. Dirty Jews!' He would beam with pleasure.

"One day he set a test for us. Quoting from a thick book, he read out, 'Scientific studies show that Aryans possess bigger skulls than other races. The bigger the skull, the bigger the brain. Inferior races, like Jews, Africans and Gypsies, possess small skulls, small brains and low foreheads, like apes. Rubbing his hands together, he produced a tape measure from his desk drawer and told us to measure each other's heads. I was certain I'd be shown up. The tape measure went round the class, Suse measuring my head, and I hers. With a smirk, the teacher asked for the results. Sizes ranged from forty-six to fifty centimetres. When he came to Suse, she read out the figure she'd jotted down, 'Hannah's head is exactly fifty centimetres, sir.'

"If looks could kill, Suse and I would both be stone dead. Luckily for us, the bell signalled the end to the lesson."

"You were lucky to have Suse stick by you." It was Pamela at the back. I was going to tell the class about my birthday party and Suse's phone message but Miss Hopkinson decided that was enough for one day, "Thank you, Hannah. I think we now know something of what it is like to go to school in Nazi Germany."

As we filed out of school, some of the children came up to me, taking my hand and saying they wanted to be my friend. On the way home with Vi and Frank, we walked along in silence across the fields, filling our sacks with rabbit food.

I wondered if they realized that for me war was anything but 'good fun'. And for me it had started before England declared war on Hitler.

Chapter Twelve

I wasn't the only one with worries about my family. Frank and Vi missed their mother and were upset when she didn't write or visit them. Now and then, Frank boasted about his father killing Germans at the front, but I could see anxiety in his eyes. Like me, he had no news.

One day, however, their mother did come to the farm. She'd sent a letter to say she was bringing some important news. Frank went around telling everyone his father had won a medal for bravery. Vi wasn't so sure.

Though Mrs Pittaway was busy with the cows when their mother finally arrived, she'd baked a sponge cake with real butter and eggs, and greengage jam filling. And she let Frank and Vi meet their mother at Havant Station. I stayed behind, waiting at the front gate.

I could hear them coming down the lane, chatting excitedly about their 'capture' of the German pilot, Frank fighting off the 'vicious' guard dog, their progress at school and regular attendance at Sunday School.

When they reached the gate, Frank introduced me to his mother. "This is Hannah, Mum. She's German. A refugee."

"But she's on our side," Vi quickly added.

The lady shook my hand with a look of kindness in her eyes. She was very kind, asking after my mama and papa, praising my English and giving me a present – a twirly orange stick of barley sugar. Mrs Pittaway and I left them alone sitting round the table, so their mother could explain why she had come.

Her news was *bad*: first their grandmother had died, then their papa had been 'killed in action.' There were floods of tears and I did my best to comfort them, giving Violet Miss Hope, my old ballerina doll and making her a daisy chain. I ironed Frank's creased shirt.

I so wanted to tell them about my own loss, how the Nazis had killed my papa too, my fears for Mama and Hans. But… somehow I couldn't get it out.

Soon after the visit, word went round the village of strange goings on. Rumour had it there was a spy in our midst. No details. Just reports that policemen had visited several homes, questioned 'suspects' and searched premises. Plain-clothes police had even been spotted up at the old manor house where Lord and Lady Bessington lived.

What they were looking for was a secret kept from the public. We were left to guess. Escaped prisoners-of-war? Spies? Collaborators? But then, what would they be doing in a sleepy English village?

One Sunday after church, we had another visit. When we were all sitting down to dinner, a loud banging interrupted Mrs Pittaway as she was saying thanks "for what we were about to receive". *No one* came between her and her Lord – as she was always telling us. She ignored the knocking. Only when she'd finished grace and opened her eyes did she get up from the table.

Even though I'd been in England three years, the sudden banging brought back instant memories of door-pounding, running feet, shouting and screaming. I sat rigidly in my chair, expecting the worst. Had the Gestapo finally caught up with me?

My fears mounted when two men in long black coats entered, asking in perfect English for "Hannah Kanel".

I nearly fainted. Oh no! A little hand under the table squeezed my fingers – it was Violet. Frank went red with confusion. Mrs Pittaway was visibly angry. She offered the men neither a seat nor a cup of tea. Instead, she turned her back on them and dug the poker into the fire, stirring up an angry shower of sparks.

That didn't please the visitors. One of them beckoned to the farmer's wife and muttered something in her ear. Silently, she led the way up the stairs to my bedroom above the kitchen. I could hear bumps and creaks and crashes; what *could* they be looking for?

Mrs Pittaway prided herself on a neat and tidy house – 'everything has its proper place in the eyes of the Lord!' – and when she re-appeared with the tall man, she let rip, giving them both a piece of her mind.

She didn't believe I was a spy and told them so in no uncertain terms, all the way to their car. I couldn't believe it when they said they were going to take me away, but that's exactly what they did. I could see Mrs Pittaway waving her arms and screaming at them.

But then I was on my own. At Emsworth police station, the secret policemen led me to a small windowless room 'for questioning'. They started with personal details: name, age, place of birth, school, religion, guardian and so on. After those formalities they got down to business. I was the only German in the village. So suspicion fell on me. My 'crime' soon became clear from their questions.

"Where's your transmitter? We know you've been sending messages to Berlin. Admit it! Where have you hidden the radio? Who is your contact? What's your code?"

Nothing I said would convince them I was innocent.

"Right," sighed the main interrogator finally. "Maybe time in the cells will refresh your memory."

Even before I was led away I heard a commotion at the front desk. A familiar voice was demanding to see the 'commanding officer'.

A policeman poked his head round the corner of the interview room. "This woman out front says she's got some information, sir."

"Could be in it together," muttered one of the officers. "Okay, bring her in. We'll charge them both."

Mrs Pittaway brought herself in, brushing off the sergeant's helping hand.

"Sit down, madam," ordered my interviewer.

"You have information for us?" said the other man.

Mrs Pittaway gathered herself together and took out her well-worn, black leather bible, covering it with both hands. "On the Holy Bible," she began in a loud voice, "my Hannah's no spy. As God's my witness."

The men wanted to intervene, but Mrs Pittaway was determined to have her say, "I'm responsible for Hannah. She's my evacuee. The girl is with me day and night – except when she's at school. If she were spying I'd be the first to know about it."

The men weren't convinced. One looked at the other before responding, "You must understand, madam, there's a war on. We can't be too careful. There are spies everywhere, however innocent they may seem. Your evacuee is German…"

Before Mrs Pittaway could reply, they stood up, "Look, let's clear this up once and for all. We'll conduct a thorough search of your farm and if we find nothing, we'll call it quits."

Chapter Thirteen

The two men drove us back to Nutbourne and, while a frightened Frank and Violet sat in the kitchen, Mrs Pittaway and I had to stand and watch as they searched the farmyard. One made for the cowshed and emerged with wisps of straw sticking to his hair and coat. Meanwhile, the other bent low to enter the chicken coop, holding his nose. I think they would have searched Rufus's kennel had his bared fangs not made them think better of it.

After a two-hour search of farm and house, they gave up in disappointment. But they weren't finished. They called everyone into the kitchen for questioning.

"Sit down, all of you," said the one with straw still in his hair. "I want you to think hard, very hard. Have you seen or heard anything suspicious, at night maybe? Anything this German might have done?"

"No!" said Mrs Pittaway, emphatically.

"How about you, girl?"

"No," said Vi in a scared whisper.

"You, boy?"

Frank's face was tense and red, his brow knitted, his lips moving as if he wished to say something, yet didn't dare.

"Come on, lad, spit it out. Your country could be in danger."

All eyes were on Frank as he finally found his voice.

"I must tell the truth," he muttered, looking down at the oilskin tablecloth. "I *have* heard Hannah talking at night in her room, and once in the cowshed. Both times in *German*."

The men leant forward eagerly, one with a pencil poised over a notepad.

"Did you catch any words?"

"Well, she often cries out at night as if in a nightmare, calling for her mother and father."

"What else? Go on."

"Once Vi and I saw her milking and she was talking to the cow. The only words I could catch were 'crystal', 'Nazi', 'Hans' and 'violin'."

"Mmm," murmured the man with the pencil, writing down the four words.

"Oh no!" said Frank, shocked. "You don't understand. She was crying for her family. I remember her saying over and over, 'Mama, Mama' and 'Oh, Papa, Papa, Papa.' She was sobbing her heart out."

At last the men turned to me. "Right, girl, what have you got to say for yourself?"

There was no choice. I had to tell them. Taking a

deep breath and holding back the tears, I said, "Papa's dead. He was murdered in a Nazi camp. He died because he stood up for others who hated Hitler. My brother Hans was taken off the train and sent back to Germany. Mama said she would join me. But, but…"

It was too much. I broke down and cried.

The silence was broken by a shout from outside. It was a uniformed police sergeant. One of the men stood up, went to the door and quickly returned. "We've found the source," he muttered. "They've located the transmitter… up at the big house."

The policemen made their apologies and left us sitting round the table in silence. No one seemed to know what to say. At last, Frank found his voice. Turning to me, he said croakily,

"Hannah, I've been wanting to say this for some time. I… I didn't know. I… I didn't understand. I'm truly, truly sorry."

Mrs Pittaway had tears in her eyes as she put the kettle on, and glancing across the table at Frank, I saw a look of true concern on his sad face.

THEN READ HANNAH

READ FRANK FIRST

FRANK'S STORY

ESCAPE FROM WAR

KINGFISHER
An imprint of Kingfisher Publications Plc
New Penderel House, 283–288 High Holborn
London WC1V 7HZ
www.kingfisherpub.com

First published by Kingfisher 2005
This edition published by Kingfisher 2006
2 4 6 8 10 9 7 5 3 1

A CIP catalogue record for this book
is available from the British Library.

ISBN-13: 978 0 7534 1354 8
ISBN-10: 0 7534 1354 X

Printed in India
1TR/0206/THOM/SGCH/80STORA/C

MY SIDE OF THE STORY

ESCAPE FROM WAR

FRANK'S STORY

JAMES RIORDAN

KINGFISHER

Read Frank's story first, then flip over
and read Hannah's side of the story!

Chapter One

Conkers started it. The war, that is.

There I was with this champion, a real beauty. I found it in the graveyard opposite our house. Or rather, it found me. Like Chicken Licken, 'the sky fell on me one morning'. Down came this leathery-spiky bomb right on my head. Ouch!

For a moment I thought Jerry had dropped one on me. 'Jerry' was our name for Germans. So there was this glossy nut winking at me from a greeny-brown case – like a dark polished pearl in an oyster shell. Right away I knew. It was my secret weapon to win the war. Taking the treasure home, I drilled a hole through its doe eye with a meat skewer, threaded it on knotted string, and sallied forth to meet the foe.

First on my calling list was Johnnie Jones next door. Now, Jonesey was a smart aleck, forever boasting of his scientifically selected conkers (and marbles, knucklebones, catapults, pea-shooters, popguns). He'd babble on about density, gravity, specific weight – that sort of twaddle. Me and my mates reckoned he soaked his conkers in vinegar and baked them in the oven – which wasn't fair.

"Hiya, Johnnie, fancy a game of conkers?" I said matter-of-factly, across the garden wall.

He peered at me suspiciously over the top of his specs.

"You're on," he said uncertainly, suspecting a trick. "I'll fetch my sixer."

He called *all* his conkers 'sixers' – to make us think they'd already claimed six victims.

I clambered over the wall from the top of our air-raid shelter to the top of his and jumped down into his garden. I had to tread carefully, to avoid Mrs Jones's neat rows of lettuce, sprouts and spuds.

As Johnnie was fetching his 'champion', I hissed at my secret weapon, "Smash his 'ead in! Punch his lights out!"

Beside my glossy beauty, the Jones conker looked dull and stone hard, like a lump of coal.

"I bags England, you're Germany," he said.

"'Snot fair."

"You started it."

"Yeah, but… You've already smashed six. I haven't done anyone."

"Oh, go on then, we'll toss for it."

All we had was a farthing between us. He flicked it up, catching it on the back of his hand.

"Heads then I choose," he called.

It was tails.

"Right, I'm England," I cried triumphantly.

"Then I bags first go," he muttered.

He couldn't help showing off, commentating into an imaginary mike as he pulled back his arm, "And the all-conquering Luftwaffe, spearheaded by fighter ace Adolf von Scheissenhofer in his Stuka dive bomber, narrows in on the target…"

He brought his conker down with a smash.

He missed.

"You moved, English swine!" he screamed. "Typical English dirty tricks!"

"No, I didn't."

"Yes, you did. I get a second go."

Nasty Nazis.

Biff! Bang! Wallop! E-n-g-l-a-n-d! Winner by a knock-out!

Johnnie's 'sixer' lay in bits on a lettuce leaf beside the footpath. Germany was a bad loser.

"You wait, Frank," he snarled as he skulked off, holding an empty piece of string. "You may have won a battle, but you won't win the war."

This had been our favourite game since the 'Big News' two weeks ago. It was quarter past eleven and we were just thinking about our Sunday roast when Grandad switched on the wireless. Just as I was walking into the kitchen, the Prime Minister, old Neville Chamberlain, had an 'Important Announcement' for us.

"Grave news... given Hitler an ultimatum... expired at noon today, the third of September nineteen thirty-nine... Hitler has not met our conditions... Consequently... *we are at war with Germany...*"

I had come back into the front room. No one really knew what to say. We had to let what we had just heard sink in. Then a voice said, "What's war?"

It was my kid sister Violet. She was only eight, two years younger than me, but as curious as a kitten.

It all went quiet again. Seven pairs of eyes – Mum's, Dad's, Auntie Dot's, Auntie Rose's, Auntie Edie's, Violet's and mine – turned to Grandad (Grandma was sick, lying on the front room couch). Grandad had been a soldier in the Great War. He had been part of the Irish Guards. Invalided out in 1917, a year before it was all over. Wheezy chest... from mustard gas or some such stuff the enemy let loose on the battlefield. He *never* talked about it.

Grandad wheezed, spat phlegm into a dirty handkerchief and cleared his throat. A low growl startled us and sent our dog Bonzo yelping off to the scullery.

"Hell!"

We were shocked. Grandad didn't allow 'blasphemy' in the house. He'd said enough for one

day. Pushing away his half-empty plate, he turned his back on us.

"What's come over Dad?" asked Auntie Rose in a hushed voice.

"The stew must've disagreed with him," said Mum. We guessed the *real* reason.

Chapter Two

Despite the 'Announcement', war hasn't come yet. Every morning's the same as the one before: no sign of war. But I still wake up in a sweat. Last night I had a dream of Germans in spiked helmets tearing down the street, jabbing bayonets into people.

Mum took me to the pictures today; it was the first time I'd seen war. Between the two cowboy films, they showed the *Pathe News*; and that shocked me rigid. It wasn't make-believe fighting. This was real. German bombs were falling on houses – there were bodies all over the place, lying in pools of blood.

What if it happened here? All we have to defend us is the Local Defence Volunteers. They are our 'secret weapon', the men behind the army who are supposed to be a ferocious band of cut-throats – trained, efficient and ruthless!

But I've seen them training and it's a joke. They are mostly dodderers too old for war, or snotty-nosed youngsters with wheezy chests, pigeon toes or a gammy leg, unfit for active service. Stick them in an army uniform, hand them a rifle… and they strut about like God Almighty, ordering people around.

My pals and I poke fun at them as they march

down the street and drill on the square outside Lipton's.

"Hey, mister, watch out you don't shoot yourself with that gun!"

If that's all we have to stand between us and Mr Hitler, God help us if Jerry does attack! Just in case he does, me and my pals get in some practice: shooting at each other, lobbing grenades, dive-bombing and falling down dead.

I listen carefully to the wireless for news of the war. It's getting closer and closer. Mum reckons Adolf Hitler wouldn't dare show his cowardly face in England. She says he's too busy at home anyway. His soldiers are going round beating up 'undesirables' – whoever they might be.

I did my bit for the war, poking fun at old Adolf. On Bonfire Night, I dressed up as Hitler instead of Guy Fawkes, with a little brush moustache and a hank of hair over one eye. Mum helped fit me up, sorting out some old clothes from the garden shed. What she didn't say was that Mrs Jones next door had tossed them out after her dad had passed on – he being the local gravedigger.

"Ugh! Phew-err!" I exclaimed, wrinkling my nose and eyes. Even Bonzo took one sniff and ran off whining.

I have to admit, it *looked* authentic – as an old beggar's outfit. Pity about the smell.

All done up as the Führer, I strutted down the street, shouting out:

"Sick Hile! Sick Hile! Penny for the Guy!"

I got a laugh and a few coppers...

Dusk was falling as I made my way home, so I took a short-cut through the cemetery. It was dead scary. What would I do if some Nazi suddenly sprang out from behind a tombstone and slit my throat? The very picture brought a nervous grin as I jogged down muddy paths. Dressed as I was, I'd be a nightmare to any poor soul I chanced upon.

"'Old yer noise," I muttered under my breath, practising what I'd say to any lurking Nazi, "or I'll slit yer throat!"

The darker it got, the more edgy I was feeling. I'd just come round the back of a broken angel when I heard a noise that sent a bundle of shivers through me.

"Oh my Gawd! It's him!" came a strangled cry. I stopped dead in my tracks, staring round. Should I make a dash for it? Only a hundred yards to go if I stepped on the grassy mounds...

"Help! It's him!"

I heard a woman's howl from behind a nearby

tombstone. So it wasn't a ghost! I don't know what got into me, instead of calling, "It's only me, missus, Frank Carter. Don't be afraid," I growled, "'Old yer noise, woman, or I'll slit yer throat!"

It must have been the clothes and all the pictures of Nazis floating around my head. Suddenly, a wild figure in a black hat and long black coat went flying down the pathway, screaming her head off, for all the world as if she'd seen a ghost. It was too late to say, "Sorry, lady, I was only joking."

At least she helped banish all thoughts of ghosts and Nazis. I fairly skipped the rest of the way, hopping over graves and vaulting the low fence into the street opposite our house.

What a relief! I soon got rid of Hitler's stinky garb, had a good wash under the cold tap and pulled on my short trousers.

That would have been the end of it… but for one thing.

"Poor old Ivy," Auntie Rose said that evening. "She got quite a turn."

Ivy was Johnnie Jones's gossipy grandma – 'Poison Ivy' we called her.

"Do you know, she was tending her Bert's grave and… what d'ya think she saw?"

No one could offer a guess.

"A ghost!"

"Get away!" said Mum.

"Yes and that isn't all. The ghost was her old Bert dressed up as Adolf Hitler!"

"Never!" said Grandad, lowering his paper.

"Must have dropped by parachute," exclaimed Auntie Edie.

"Heaven, more like it," said Mum. "Her Bert's been dead these last ten years."

"How could she tell it was him?" asked Auntie Dot.

"Oh, it was him, all right. No mistaking the black 'tash and evil face. And he was wearing Bert's clothes."

Suddenly, I was seized by a fit of coughing, as if I had a fish bone in my throat. All eyes turned to me.

"You okay, son?" asked Mum, giving me a hard stare. "You'd better go and have a drink of water."

I couldn't wait to escape out the back door.

Chapter Three

A letter arrived at number thirty-nine George Street this morning. An *official* letter in a long brown envelope, with four black letters in the top left-hand corner: OHMS – On His Majesty's Service. *Blimey!*

It was so 'official' that the postman rapped on the door to hand it to me in person. Gran, Vi and I were the only ones home.

"Hello, Frank. Call-up papers," he said grimly.

"Oh, I'm too young," I replied breezily.

"Nah, not you, son. Your dad. He is Albert Harold Carter, ain't he?"

Without waiting for an answer, he said, "Sign on the dotted line."

I scrawled *Frank Carter* on a slip of paper, in exchange for the envelope.

"Ta, mate," said the postman, moving on to next door. He wouldn't get much joy there: no one round our way had ever set eyes on Mr Jones.

"Who was it, Frank?" came a croaky voice from the front room.

"Postie, Gran. Call-up papers for Dad."

"Golly."

I glanced at the mantelpiece clock ticking busily away. Five to nine! Better make a dash for it: I didn't

want to be late for school. I slicked my hair down with tap water, pulled on my flannel jacket over my grey pullover and rushed out of the house. Oh no! I had forgotten my gas mask! Back I rushed for it.

"Bye, Gran, see you at dinner time."

Luckily, I only had to sprint down the road to George Street Elementary School. Just in time. My class was filing into the hall as I tagged on the back. It was Friday, so the chatter was loud and excited. Once we were sitting cross-legged on the hall's wooden floor, however, the twittering ceased as if cut with a knife.

Infants took up the front rows, seven-to-nines the middle, and us ten-getting-on-for-eleven-year-old juniors the back.

Our class teachers were sitting, backs straight, on wooden chairs down the side, keeping a beady eye on trouble makers and gossips. Once we were all settled, the doors opened and six senior teachers marched in, slowly climbed the steps to the platform and stood, hands folded, in a row at the back. Everyone was waiting for the Headmaster.

You could have heard a pin drop as the doors flew open and in swept Mr White, a thin, lanky figure, blue-chinned and bald-headed. He marched briskly up to the platform, mounted the steps and took his

place at the front, like a vicar about to deliver a sermon.

No smiles. Shiny bald head glowing pink. Three-piece black suit and tie. Old 'Chalky' glowered about him, his bushy ginger eyebrows jogging up and down, his little grey eyes boring into every forehead.

Waiting impatiently for coughers and nose-blowers to finish, the Head twitched his shoulders, peered over the top of his spectacles and gripped the sides of the lectern with both hands.

"Silence!" he shrieked. That worked its usual charm.

A deathly hush came over the hall as all eyes were on the fierce beetle-browed figure. His face was bluer and his head redder than usual. We could tell that Chalky was about to descend on us like a ton of bricks. We all searched our minds for mischief he might have found out about. Boys caught smoking Woodbines in the toilets? Girls chalking hopscotch squares on his nice clean playground? Heads to be examined for nits?

"SCHOOL! War has begun!"

Oh, is that all? Had Chalky only just heard?

"We must all do our bit. Together we shall stop Mr Hitler in his tracks. He and his bully boys want to take over the world. But we won't let him, do you hear?

We didn't know whether to shout: "No-o-o-o!" as at the Christmas pantomime, or keep silent. We kept silent. Chalky was doing his best imitation of Mr Churchill, the Prime Minister, with bulldog face and snarling voice.

"Why are we at war? To defend liberty, that's why! To defend these islands of ours from being trampled on by German jackboots. To defend the Empire. Rule Britannia!"

"Three monkeys up a stick, one fell down and broke his... Rule Britannia..." It was a girl's voice behind me, loud enough to set us off sniggering.

Chalky jumped as if stung. "Silence! You, boy! What did you say?" His long bony finger pointed in our direction.

"Mr Cleal! Fetch that boy out. I'll not have idle chatter in my school. Loose talk costs lives!"

Mr Cleal jumped up like a scalded cat at the end of our row, desperately trying to follow the Head's finger. Some boy – it *had* to be a boy – was going to pay.

"You, Whiteway!"

"Me, sir? No, sir. Not me, sir!"

"Yes it was! I saw you. You're always talking in assembly. Get out!"

Amid the lull in the storm, poor 'Cider' Whiteway

scrambled to his feet and walked guiltily out of the hall – to join Sam Rubinstein in the classroom. Sam always sat out assemblies because his parents didn't hold with Christian hymns and prayers.

"Now then," snarled the Headmaster. "Where was I? Oh, yes, our brave boys are going off to fight the foe. George Street Old Boys, your fathers and older brothers perhaps; they've received their call-up papers. Off to serve King and Country. Bless 'em all! Once in France they'll soon scuttle the cowardly foe!"

A flicker of a smirk passed quickly over his face – a rare crack in the smooth façade of authority.

"The Germans are all swine, a nation of blackguards, not to be trusted."

Behind him Mr Bonhofer shuffled uneasily, his face reddening with shame at being tainted with the blood of German 'blackguards'. (His grandfather came from Berlin.)

The Headmaster had said enough for the moment. Nodding to Mrs Horseman at the piano below him, he led the first hymn of the day. No one sang louder than poor Mr Bonhofer, his out-of-tune voice soaring up to the rafters, as if to prove he was more English than anyone present.

To everyone's surprise, as the hymn came to an

19

end, an odd gurgle issued from the Head's throat. Mrs Horseman and the platform teachers were caught out. Eventually, they recognised the national anthem and, with the entire assembly, stood to attention. But they were always a word or two behind Chalky. As we all filed out of the hall I overheard Mr Bonhofer hiss in old Mr Steed's ear, "It's a *German* tune anyway!"

On our way home from school, Sam Rubinstein hurried to keep pace with Violet and me. He lived at the other end of our terrace; his dad ran a shop on the main road.

No one much liked him. Not attending Religious Instruction or morning assembly made him different. Some wondered whose side he was on. His name sounded foreign, German even. And he stared at you – not goggle-eyed exactly – but as if his sad black eyes saw some terrible tragedy about to break. No wonder some kids called him names, like 'Jew boy'.

"Whose side are you on, Sam?" Violet asked.

She was always asking awkward questions.

He stared at her as if she'd asked why he had two heads. Then he said, going all red, "Ours, of course."

"Yeah," I added in support of my sister, "that's as may be, but you're not one of us, are you?"

"'Course I am!"

"You're a Jew boy."

He went quiet, kicking a bald tennis ball up against a wall as we wandered home.

"Jesus was a Jew boy," he murmured.

What a cheek! Jesus was *ours*. He couldn't be a Jew boy, could he?

Chapter Four

Dad had to go away for a fortnight to do what they called 'basic training'. Mum saw him off on the train to Aldershot Barracks. When he came home, we hardly recognized him. He walked through the door at tea time, all done up in uniform. Very smart. Khaki jacket and trousers, stiff round hat under his arm and shiny black boots. What remained of his mousy brown hair was all smoothed down as if someone had sat on his head.

"Harold!" shrieked Mum when she saw him, spitting crumbs all over the table. Vi and I rushed to hug him. Even Grandad's stern face creased in a smile.

"I haven't got long," said Dad. "Weekend pass. Off to fight the good fight on Monday morning."

Saturday and Sunday raced by – football, pictures, Sunday school, walks along the river, long conversations about what we'd do after the war... Then he was off again.

On Monday morning, Grandad, Mum, Vi and I walked to the railway station with Dad. Vi and I walked proudly at his side, both trying to be the one to hold his free hand. He was holding a kitbag on one shoulder with his other hand. In his smart uniform he

looked so handsome, attracting admiring glances from passing girls.

Grandad seemed more talkative than usual, perhaps remembering the day he marched away to war. Mum was silent, lost in thought. As we drew closer to the station, we joined up with other soldiers and sailors and their families. On each corner crowds were waving and clapping. I was so scared I'd get lost in the crowd, I clung on tightly to Dad's hand.

Voices called,

"Good luck, boys."

"Cheerio, lads."

"Come back soon."

To my surprise, I heard an elderly woman in a black hat strike a different note. "Poor beggars. Fancy sending them to their deaths."

Dad must have heard her too. He glared in her direction, looking as if he wanted to shout in her ear, "I'm not going to die, for you or anyone else!"

At the station, Mum flung her arms round him, and out gushed the unblocked stream of tears. She *had* heard the moaning minnie along the way for she suddenly mumbled through her sobs, "If you don't come back…"

Impatiently, Dad stopped her before she could finish.

"Don't fret, love, it'll be all over by Christmas."

He bent down to give Violet and me a kiss. I squeezed his hand and said, "I'll look after the rabbits, Dad."

Grandad simply said, "Good luck, lad," and turned quickly away.

So Dad marched off to war with thousands of others. And I cried my eyes out at night.

Chaper Five

Christmas is here now. Why isn't Dad back? He promised. We're wondering why we haven't had a letter. Auntie Rose said, "He's enjoying himself too much. All them ooh-la-la French gals…" I could guess what 'ooh-la-la' means from the wink my aunt gave her sisters. She didn't dare repeat it in front of Mum.

Now that Dad is on 'active service' over there, we're hungry for scraps of information. Fighting was going on in far-away places, so far away they seemed off the end of the world.

Then, all at once, the Germans attacked. They waited until it was dark and we'd all gone to bed. The air-raid siren wailed. We tumbled out of bed, raced down the stairs, out into the garden, down into the air-raid shelter. Fingers crossed the bombs wouldn't fall on us.

Not that crossed fingers and legs helped much. Auntie Rose reckons that every bomb has someone's name chalked on it. No matter what you do, it'll get you. I imagined a great big bomb with 'Frank' written on it, twirling down, looking for me – "Frank, I'm coming to get you!" – and landing on my head. I felt quite a thrill sitting in the shelter,

huddled together with Mum, Vi, my aunties, Bonzo and Grandad. Gran was too poorly to get to the shelter.

I was half asleep, waiting for the 'all-clear' so I could stagger back to my nice warm bed. All at once, however, Auntie Dot let out a scream as if she'd been shot, "Tiddles!"

Bonzo growled at the mere mention of the cat's name.

"We've forgotten the cat!"

Tiddles is our tabby tom, a battle-scarred veteran of many a scrap. He guards his territory better than the Home Guard does the English coast. He was not even afraid of No. 35's Ginger – commonly known as 'Adolf'.

"Hasn't Gran got him?" sighed Auntie Rose.

"No, I checked."

Auntie Dot cared more for that cat than she did for herself. She was always putting on damp vests, yet she regularly aired the cat's blanket and took him into bed with her, fleas or no fleas.

"I'm going to look for him."

"You can't," said Mum. "There's a raid on. They could drop a bomb on you, then you'd be sorry."

Auntie Dot stood up, her head bent beneath the corrugated roof.

"I'm going," she repeated, a bit uncertainly, as if she expected someone to talk her out of it.

"Go on, then," said Auntie Rose. "But don't come crying to us if you get your head blown off!"

Pulling the curtain aside, Auntie Dot poked her head out, listened to the guns going off and the droning planes. Then, in a gap in the gunfire, she started calling, "Tiddles, Tiddles! Come on, old fella."

She started quietly, as if German pilots might hear her. Then, when Tiddles didn't come, she shouted more loudly.

I knew Tiddles hated the air-raid shelter. Whether it was the stinking sandbags or the foot-deep rainwater, God knows. But he probably preferred to take his chances underneath the rabbit hutch or garden shed, risking one of his nine lives in the open where he could make a dash for it.

"There's nothing for it," grunted Auntie Dot. "I'll have to brave the bombs."

By this time her sisters were ready to call her bluff.

"Go on then, silly," called Auntie Rose. "And pull the flap to after you or Adolf'll see our oil lamp."

Auntie Dot has always been as stubborn as a mule. She wasn't going to back down now. Clumsily, she stepped out of the shelter, letting the flap fall back into place. We could hear her blundering down the

garden, cursing "Oh, damn!" as she caught her nightie on the brambles.

That brought Grandad to life. He bellowed loud enough for the enemy to hear, "Watch your language!"

It all went quiet. No longer could we hear her footsteps or timid calls of, "Tiddles, Tiddles, Tiddles…" After a few minutes we all began to fear for her safety.

"Where do you think she's got to?" asked Mum.

"Likely some Jerry's grabbed her," muttered Auntie Edie. "You know, parachuted down, nabbed her and taken her back to Germany."

"No!"

It was little Vi come to life.

"What, our Auntie Dot?"

"What'll they do with her?" I asked, half believing our auntie was a prisoner of the Germans.

"Oh, the usual," murmured Auntie Edie. "Thumb screws, Chinese burns, red-hot needles under her toenails."

"She could give our secrets away," gasped my sister. "Our names. Where we live. Where we go to school, our hiding places. We've had it!"

"Not your Auntie Dot," said Mum gravely. "More likely, she'll make them talk, and they'll end up sending her home, glad to be rid of her."

Mum was right, she normally is. Just then we heard Auntie Dot's fairy footsteps crashing down the alleyway at the side of the house. It sounded like she'd caught a savage tiger what with the snarls, growls and hisses as she brought a very unwilling tabby with her.

She appeared in the shelter doorway, holding Tiddles by the scruff of the neck.

"Do you know where he was, the scallywag?"

Without waiting for our guesses, she told us as she splashed through the rainwater.

"Only billing and cooing with some black she-cat under a bush across the road, that's what."

Tiddles wasn't at all pleased to have his love life nipped in the bud, even if there was a war on. He growled his displeasure. As Auntie Edie sat him on her lap, ruffling his mangy fur, the 'all-clear' went. Thankfully, we climbed back upstairs to bed, first making sure Gran was all right.

The same routine happens every night. It's scary waiting for the droning noise of the warplanes, staring up, not knowing whether the buzzing mosquitoes overhead will turn out to be *ours* or *theirs*.

We needn't have worried. Winter and spring have passed and no bombs have fallen on our neighbourhood.

Jerry celebrated my eleventh birthday on 10 April

by sending over lots of planes. Someone must have counted them because the papers reckoned they saw exactly three hundred bombers and six hundred fighters. Once they started arriving, boy did they come thick and fast: dive bombers, Heinkels, Junkers and Dorniers. How they didn't bump into each other in the dark, I'll never know. The sky was simply thick with them, like a swarm of flying ants.

Old Clever Clogs Jones next door reckoned he could spot the plane by the sound of its engine. "The Stukas make a high-pitched whine, like the Heinkel HE 1-11. Not to be confused with the Junker and Dornier Flying Pencil bombers. They're dead easy to spot from their cranked wings and flat undercarriages, like coffin lids. Remember that, Frank. Your life may depend on it one day!"

Cocky blighter.

Chapter Six

It's beginning to rain bombs. There are so many
explosions and fires you'd think the heavens were
ablaze. People are calling it the Blitz. More like a
terrible storm, with thunder and lightning in the sky
and the fires of hell below. Mind you, unless you get
blown to bits, it's quite good fun; more exciting than
moving pictures at the Odeon.

We usually get a warning. First the siren climbs to
a high-pitched whine. Then an eerie silence: the lull
before the storm. Next a distant drone of bombers
growing louder and louder until the noise is
deafening, like a swarm of violent, angry bees.

Soon after, someone switches on the sky lights. It's
more brilliant than Bonfire Night. The heavens
instantly come alive with white searchlights, criss-
crossing the sky against a backdrop of twinkling stars
and a pale crescent moon. And then… the strangely
cheerful booming noise of Bofors guns punctured by
the death rattle of machine guns, like someone
running an iron spike along the cemetery railings.

Then another brief hush, then quite a different
sound. Peering out of the shelter I silently cheer a
flight of Spitfires or Hurricanes, thundering up the
sky to intercept the foe. Holding my breath, I watch

the deadly dogfight, a battle against time: Defenders versus Attackers. But, in the boundless night sky, *nothing* can halt each and every German plane. There are too many of them. It's like firing a pea-shooter at a great cloud of gnats.

Puffs of red and orange smoke light up the heavens as shells explode all round the attacking planes. A brilliant white spray of tracer bullets arcs upwards, intersecting the purple-scarlet shots from the ground. But you can't shine a light on every bomber carrying a black cross. It's like trying to spot a moth in the candlelight of a darkened room.

As the bombers close in on their target, the ominous drone gives way to a high-pitched whine, like Grandad snoring.

The best bit was when I actually saw a direct hit – ours or theirs, I couldn't tell, but I always imagined it was an enemy plane hurtling down: an exploding fire-cracker bursting into fiery red sparks and a ball of metal and fire spiralling round and round like a falling sycamore seed.

I held my breath until it hit the ground and I heard a thud and thought of the cloud of white smoke climbing skywards, piercing the dark sky.

Next day Violet and I went searching for trophies in the cemetery opposite and then in the bluebell

woods at the back of the recreation ground – maybe a spent bullet case or chunk of shrapnel. German trophies are the ones most prized at school: leather flying helmets, cigarette packets, a swastika badge.

But we never found a sausage! Still, we had lots of fun, scaring the living daylights out of one another, especially in the graveyard. I hid behind a tombstone and jumped out, shouting, *"Handy Hoch!"* or *"Nein, nein, hang your breeches on the line!"*

That night a high-explosive bomb flattened a row of houses a few streets away. We aren't supposed to enter bombed houses. Too dangerous. But the air-raid wardens had more urgent jobs than chasing nosey kids. So Violet and I went exploring.

To tell the truth, we were dead scared, holding hands for comfort. Our hearts were in our mouths as we poked around in the rubble, half expecting to stumble upon a dead body or, worse still, torn-off arms or bloody leg stumps. Up the rickety stairs we went, with dust and soot poking their smelly fingers into our noses and mouths. To stop ourselves choking, we had to hold our breath and press hankies to our faces.

I don't know what we expected to find: a grubby Snakes and Ladders or Ludo board, pack of cards, some tiddlywinks or cigarette cards. We searched both

bedrooms, finding only two halves of an old chamber pot, a tennis ball and an unopened jar of quince jam.

Under some bricks we discovered a photo album with pictures of a soldier in smart uniform smiling out; a family of six, staring seriously at the camera, sitting bolt upright; a little baby, lying on its tummy, all done up in a woolly romper and a sailor hat.

Then it happened. Just as we were going down the wobbly stairs, we heard it. A snarl from below.

"Who's dat up dere?"

We froze. Could it be a Nazi desperado?

"I'm coming to get you!" came a rough voice.

Our hair stood on end and our knees were knocking; we thought our end had come. Should we shout down, '*Creamers! We give in.*'?

Suddenly, we heard a belly laugh. And there was Eric Eddles, one of my schoolmates, giggling his head off. He'd seen us go in and decided to give us a fright. He certainly did that all right!

Chapter Seven

Something happened that put a stop to our explorations. The family (apart from Gran, who refused to budge from her front room) was sitting in our air-raid shelter, huddled together, with blankets round us to keep warm. We were half asleep, waiting for the 'all-clear'.

All of a sudden there came a blast so violent it rammed my eardrums through my skull, rattled every bone in my body and pinned me against the corrugated-iron wall. The ground shook beneath my feet as from an earthquake, splashing smelly water over my welly tops and down to my feet. Had the world come to an end?

I imagined the house tumbling about my ears – I could certainly hear crashing and the tinkling of shattered glass as our windows were blown out. It seemed to be raining stones. The council men were right: our air-raid shelter did come in handy. Thuds and pings rang out above us. A hot stone or something came hurtling through the doorway, making a hole in the curtain that hung there; then the missile sizzled and fizzed in the rainwater puddles on the floor.

If it wasn't the end of the world, it had to be a bomb. And that bomb must have fallen on our house;

the blast was too deafening to come from anywhere else. We were certain we'd find our cosy brick home as flat as a pancake. I was biting my fingernails down to the quick. We hardly dared look. We were thinking of Gran, none of us daring to say the worst had happened.

The first to move was Tiddles. He shot out of the shelter like a bat out of hell, scratching aside the singed curtain. That cat did us all a favour.

For we could then see that, apart from fallen slates and broken glass glittering in the moonlight, our house was still standing. We could smell fire and smoke. Yet we saw no flames. The tornado had passed and my eardrums, though still popping, were regaining their hearing. Was that someone hollering and screaming in the distance?

Soon after, the welcome wail of the siren announced the 'all-clear'. It dropped down to a low wail, as if running out of puff. It was a bit like a gramophone when the needle slows down and you have to wind it up again.

"There's nothing we can do in the dark," said Auntie Edie. "If anyone's wounded or trapped, the ambulances will take care of them."

Ignoring her own words, she went inside to get dressed and go off to see if her First Aid skills could

come in handy. The rest of us followed Grandad upstairs, while Mum went to have a word with Gran, who was okay apart from a bad headache.

Next morning I awoke with a start. For a split second I panicked: was I late for school? The room was still dark. It took me a while to realize that someone had rigged up a makeshift paper black-out over the window to cover the broken glass. Then I remembered: it was Saturday. Football down the park, marbles in the gutter, and conker searches in the cemetery. Then, all at once, last night's bomb came to mind.

"Vi," I cried. "Saturday. Adventure time! Hunting for dead Germans."

"Oh no you don't!" came Mum's voice from downstairs. "Not with unexploded bombs about. There could also be Jerries around, dropped in the night, waiting to pounce on you."

The tone of her voice softened. "I'm thinking of packing you two kiddies off to safety. Evacuation. That's what the government advises."

"Eee-vac-kew-ay-shun!" I'd heard that strange word at school. It sent shivers through me. A couple of my friends, Frank Harfield and Johnnie Lee, had disappeared before the Blitz started, as 'evacuees', never to be seen again, some people said. I didn't like the sound of that at all.

"We're safe with you, Mum," I called down. "What with Dad gone, you need a man to look after you."

I don't think that convinced her. But for the moment she said no more about it.

Chapter Eight

After breakfast, Mum, Vi and I ventured out of doors, well wrapped up in scarves and coats against the bitter wind. The sights and smells that greeted us were ominous. All along the street we crunched our way through broken glass and bits of brick and roof slate. Most chimneys were skew-whiff, and the musty smell of brick dust tickled our noses.

We could see above the roof tops a dark pall of spiralling smoke, rising into the pale autumn sky.

Luckily, it started to rain, a fine drizzle. That would, hopefully, put a damper on any fires and stop them spreading to our house.

"Come on, kids," called Mum, hurrying us up. "Looks like the next road."

We had no idea what awaited us or what we might have to do to help.

When we reached the corner, we stopped dead in our tracks, staring at the scene opposite in Shearer Road. It resembled a boxer with his front teeth knocked out.

There were numbers twenty-seven and twenty-nine... then... thirty-five!

Where had thirty-one and thirty-three gone?

Number thirty-one had disappeared off the face of

the earth. So had half of number thirty-three. So that's what last night's terrible noise was! I couldn't get it into my head how twenty feet of upstairs and downstairs had collapsed into one foot of rubble!

The closer we came to the gaping hole in the row of houses, the more smoking, plum-coloured bricks and shards of glass we had to step over. The front bedroom wall of number thirty-three was missing; it reminded me of the doll's house Dad made for Violet last Christmas, with its front removed.

The moment I looked up, I felt embarrassed, as if I'd caught someone lying in bed in their nightie! I could feel myself blushing a beetroot red.

Number thirty-one must have taken a direct hit. How else would it have gone up in smoke, bringing thirty-three down with it?

"It's poor Mr and Mrs Weller," said Mum. Her hand covered her mouth in horror at the awful thought they might be dead.

"Where have they gone, Mum?" asked Violet in a tiny voice.

"Let's hope they made it to the shelter," she replied anxiously.

"They did," came a woman's voice behind us. "See that big crater in the garden?"

"You don't mean…?"

"'Fraid so. God bless their souls. Hardly a scrap of flesh and bone left to bury. At least they wouldn't have known much about it, eh?"

"Best way to go," remarked Mum, taking out her hanky and having a snivel.

"Same as the Browns at thirty-one," continued the woman, glad to find someone to talk to. "All four of the poor devils. Caught the blast full on. Must have been a big 'un, one of them high explosives or flying bombs. They blow you to kingdom come, you know."

"You don't say!"

"Someone says they're still there, underneath all that rubble. Burnt to a frazzle, most likely, what with the blaze. Still searching for what's left of 'em."

"Gorblimey!"

"Funny thing is, I was only having a chinwag with Betty Brown at the butcher's yesterday morning. She looked in the pink... who'd have thought, eh? Shame about all that meat she bought with her coupons. Wasted now. Anyway, she was saying how they were thinking of sending the kids away to the country, somewhere nice and safe."

Mention of 'the kids' sent shivers through me. Those 'kids' were Eric Eddles, the one who'd scared us in that bombed house, and his sister Maisie! They'd been adopted by the Browns before the war.

No, I couldn't believe it. *Not* Eric and Maisie. I could see his cheeky grin as if he were standing in front of me right now, giving me a suck of his green gobstopper. His kid sister was in the class below Violet; she had freckles all over her face, and red hair so fiery you could burn your fingers on it.

I gazed at the broken house, thinking of Eric and Maisie; I scarcely noticed the hot tears rolling down my cheeks. I remembered Dad. If he was fighting at the front, was he seeing worse than this? What *could* be worse than this?

To banish thoughts of Eric, I squinted up at the open bedroom. I made out a picture of the King, hanging lopsidedly on the far wall. It was still in its cracked frame. Despite the smoky smashed glass, King George was still smiling shyly, as if to say, "Keep your spirits up!"

In the empty space where the outside wall had been was a cast-iron bedstead covered in bricks and beams instead of sheets and pillows, bolster and eiderdown. Its back legs were dangling over the edge, swaying to and fro in the breeze. It could come crashing down at any moment. Raindrops were splashing the bluebell wallpaper on the open sides of the room.

We watched, fascinated, as wardens in white tin

hats dug with shovels and bare hands in the ruins of what yesterday had been two neat and tidy homes. An ambulance was standing by a few doors down, its woman driver staring disconsolately at the smoking rubble, waiting to carry off whatever remained.

Amidst the broken cups and plates, the groceries and spilled cigarettes, the scattered white sugar and flour, we could make out items that had obviously fallen through a hole in the ceiling: someone's baggy underpants and a big beige bra draped over the black stove; a cracked chamber pot standing upright like a flower vase on the table.

That was inside. But the blast had also blown personal belongings into the road and all over the pavement where they didn't belong. Bottles of brown vinegar had smashed, spilling out onions like dead eyeballs and leaving a sour smell in the road. It made your eyes smart.

It wasn't long before the ambulance woman was summoned. She brought a stretcher from the vehicle, carrying it towards a hole the diggers had made. We saw her staring down into the rubble as a warden, feet apart, pulled up what looked like a sack of potatoes.

The woman bustled back over the ruins, opened the ambulance door and pulled out a second stretcher, carrying it rolled up by its two poles.

For the next half hour, several hands heaved bricks and broken furniture to one side, making the tunnel bigger, until they could drag out whatever they'd discovered.

"Don't look!" ordered Mum.

Like a mouse before a snake, we just couldn't look away. Although we didn't actually see any bodies, we knew *something* awful was being pulled out and laid on the stretchers. The helpers stretched blankets over the 'find' to hide it from view.

At last, the bulky ambulance woman took the pole ends in her hands, while a warden bent down to grip the other end. "Ready?" she called out. "On the count of three, lift… one… two… three!"

They lifted up the lumpy stretcher and moved gingerly over the rubble towards the ambulance, passing within an arm's length of us.

The blanket didn't quite cover it up. Naked grey legs poked out at one end. A pair of feet were still wearing dusty brown carpet slippers. When they brought out a second body, the feet were bare, its ugly toes as stiff as tombstones.

They were the first dead bodies I'd ever seen. Well, dead feet at least – that's bad enough.

As we walked away, Violet whispered to Mum, "That bomb must have had their names on it."

"Yes, love," Mum replied. "Oh, Frank, don't cry, love. Come here."

"I'm not crying, Mum, I'm *not* crying."

Chapter Nine

The Blitz is getting worse by the day – or rather, night. Not a single night-time goes by without a raid. None of us get much sleep. Even the teachers at school are yawning their heads off. Poor Mr Steed fell asleep at his desk one day as we were scratching away with our pen nibs. He must have had a shock when he woke up to find the classroom empty: we'd all tiptoed out to play!

Almost all the younger schoolmasters have joined up. Not Chalky, of course – worse luck. He was let off, he let it be known, for a higher calling: his mission was to lick us into shape, make men of us (even the girls).

"In these dark times," he thundered, "when our great land is under attack, I have resolved to turn this school into a parade ground – for drilling future soldiers... and, uh, mothers of soldiers. You will learn to obey without question."

Poor Chalky never did get his wish to turn our school into a parade ground. One night soon after, a fire bomb fell on the school and burned it to the ground. I reckon we must have had a spy among us – I had my eye on Sam Rubinstein – who'd sent a coded message to Hitler, giving away Chalky's plans.

Not that the burning down of the school put paid

to our schooling. No such luck. We were herded into the church hall and divided up among draughty rooms. Since there were no inkwells or desks, we went back to the Stone Age and used chalk and slate.

Our school wasn't the only building to burn down. Some places were getting hit two or three times over – bit of a waste of bombs, really. Sometimes the entire sky was ablaze, reflecting the raging fires, swirling ash, belching smoke – all the destruction on the ground, heaven turned to hell! It got so bad you'd think those incendiaries would set fire to the heavens themselves, with God and all his angels. Know-all Jones was positive the snowflakes that drifted down at Christmas were bits of fluff from burnt angel wings.

On Saturday morning I saw the telegraph boy from our upstairs window; he was cycling down our road, whistling. "Don't stop at number thirty-nine!" I whispered under my breath. Oh no! He came straight to our door. It almost finished Gran off, just the sight of the navy-blue red-piped uniform and red bike. As I opened the door, the boy shouted cheerily,

"Telegram for Mrs Wiggins."

"What is it?" croaked Gran from the front room.

"It's all right, Gran," I called back. "Wrong house."

"Over the road, mate," I said to the boy. "Number thirty-eight."

We were spared… this time. But not for long. A letter arrived for 'Miss D. Smith'. When Auntie Dot came home from her munitions work, she opened it up at the tea table, read a few lines to herself, put it down beside her plate and carried on eating as if nothing had happened.

Now, any letter was a rarity in our house. And when one came, it was shared among everyone. But this was war. Nobody asked questions. The opened letter was left for Grandad, when he came home from sweeping chimneys. He wasn't pleased to see the torn envelope. When he read the contents, he glared at Auntie Dot and growled, "Do they know about your Jack?"

Jack is her fiancé, he's in the Royal Navy, serving on minesweepers.

"No."

"Shall I read it out?"

"Please yourself, Dad."

In the hush, Grandad read out the letter from Jack's mother in Grimsby.

Dear Doris,

Sorry to send bad news. I enclose a telegram we've just received.

Yours truly,
Mary Mason

That's all. Grandad took off his glasses, wiped them on his waistcoat and put them on again to read out the telegram. We could see it was in block letters.

HMS STIRLING CAME UNDER ENEMY ATTACK AT 0200 HOURS ON 11 MAY STOP SHE SANK WITH THE LOSS OF ALL HANDS STOP ABLE SEAMAN JACK MASON IS MISSING PRESUMED DEAD STOP

We were in shock, but Auntie Dot showed no emotion. She hung a photo of her Jack in his naval uniform over the bed.

"When this lot's over and done with," she said, "we can grieve properly."

She's a hard nut, my Auntie Dot.

Chapter Ten

The Blitz doesn't ever stop... night after night after night. On and on and on and on...

Where do those Jerries get all the planes, pilots and bombs? No matter how many we shoot down, even more come over the next night. Surely they have to run out of men and aeroplanes soon!

Sometimes I can even see the bombs falling – like black blobs of deadly rain. Thousands upon thousands. Just think: each bomb can kill a crowd of innocent people. Now, if one bomb kills, say, ten people, how many would a thousand bombs account for? And how long would it take to wipe out the whole population of London? I didn't want to think about it.

The papers are saying kids would be safer out of town, away from air-raids – somewhere quiet in the country. I don't want to go. I don't want to leave Mum and Gran and my aunties. And I certainly don't want to be sent away with my sister, who's forever whining and telling tales. But Mum sat Vi and me down and told us in a very grave voice, "It's all settled."

We were to be *evacuated*. That dreaded word.

"Government orders," said Mum. She was always blaming the government.

I moaned and groaned, sniffled and groused, promised to be good, always. But it made no difference. If the government said you'd got to go, you'd got to go. We were dressed up in our Sunday best, handed a packed lunch and had a piece of cardboard pinned to our coats with our names on – like dogs with collars. Last but not least, we had to tie the hated gas masks round our necks.

After I'd said goodbye to Dad's rabbits, Bonzo and Tiddles, Gran and Grandad and our aunties, Mum took us by trolley bus to Waterloo Station. There we joined a swirling stream of other 'evacuees', some crying their eyes out, some looking lost and miserable, some chattering excitedly, all flowing towards various platforms.

What with all the bomb damage, we had to take pot luck with trains. The railway station was also crowded with men in uniform – sailors and airmen as well as soldiers, all being fussed over by tearful women in smart outfits and tilted hats with kids clinging to their skirts.

We were being sent to a farm in a village called Nutbourne, somewhere down on the south coast, away from the 'action'. Having asked a guard about platforms and times, Mum handed us one-way tickets and bundled us onto our train. Like the platform, the

train was packed with servicemen. They looked so young. But they were very polite, giving up their seats to us in a third-class compartment. Vi and I got to sit by the window, which we wound down so that Mum could give us last-minute instructions — for the millionth time.

"Get off at Havant Station. Mrs Pittaway will be waiting to pick you up. Be polite. Don't be cheeky to anyone, Frank! And don't bite your nails."

As an afterthought, she said strictly, "And don't talk to strangers on the train... they could be spies."

Violet started crying, setting Mum and me off. Just then, the train jolted and clanged, let out steam and, with a huge sigh, we were off.

"I'll be down soon," shouted Mum, disappearing like a genie in a cloud of smoke, "be good!"

Anxiously we watched the platform recede farther and farther into the distance, as if *it* was moving, not us. I gazed out at the sights of London as the train chugged out of the station.

Nothing could have prepared me for what I saw. I'd heard on the wireless about the London Blitz, but we were never told what had been bombed. For the first time I was actually seeing the mess for myself. Empty black shells that had once been blocks of flats, with abandoned swings and slides in the gardens below.

Burnt-out chapels and churches, with tottering spires and smashed stained-glass windows, toppled tombstones and fallen angels. Mile upon mile of smoking rubble that had once been houses where families had lived, children had been born and grown up. Where were they now?

Banks and offices, shops and pubs, fire stations and bus depots… A police station had disappeared off the face of the earth, leaving a lone blue lamp swinging in the breeze.

It is as if a giant has trampled across the land, crushing everything in his path, stamping on buses and carts, lampposts and buildings… people… anything that gets in his way.

Why? It didn't make any sense. The clickety-clack of wheels over sleepers turned into angry chants in my head, *"Kill a Jerry! Kill a Jerry! – You'll pay for this! You'll pay for this! – Adolf's a swine! Adolf's a swine!"*

Since I was now officially 'head of the family' (as Mum said), it was my duty to look after Violet. She was sitting and sobbing quietly in one corner of the compartment, with me squeezed in beside her and two other boys. Three girls were sitting opposite with a long-faced woman who sat bolt upright on the edge of her seat – as if she didn't want to catch anyone's

fleas. She obviously had no time for snivellers because, all at once, she said sharply, "Stop that noise!"

Even when Violet's weeping died to a whimper, it didn't satisfy the woman in the blue hat and feather. Her dark eyes bored into both of us like a hand drill, highly disapproving. Her thin lips moved like a goldfish grabbing fish-food, as a tut-tut-tut slipped out. Finally, she snapped, "Think of our soldiers in the war. Be brave, girl!"

Vi apparently did think of our brave soldiers, including Dad. After a few more watery sighs, she turned off the waterworks.

No one was in the mood to play 'I spy' or 'noughts and crosses', or even to chat about our journey into the unknown. Each girl and boy sat with their own gloomy thoughts, hating every clickety-click that took them farther away from home. None of us looked forward to being safe and sound in the country. Give us our mothers and families in London any day, bombs or no bombs!

The two boys left us at Haslemere, the three girls at Petersfield. No one said goodbye. The next stop was Havant. As the train drew into the station I could hear seagulls squawking. I'd never been to the seaside. I couldn't even swim – there wasn't room in our bath-tub.

"Ha-a-vant! Ha-a-vant! All change for Hayling Island!"

Clutching our gas masks, my sister and I stepped down from the train. A wiggly line of children was winding its way reluctantly towards the exit, their pasty faces staring fearfully at the waiting crowd. A guard added to the panic by blowing his whistle and waving a green flag, sending our train chug-chug-chugging towards Portsmouth Harbour in clouds of smoke.

"Welcome to Hampshire, matey," he said chummily to me and patted Vi on the head.

"Cheer up, missy. Worse things happen at sea. You're *safe* now."

Safe or not, we both missed home sweet home. We handed our tickets to a man in a peaked cap and dark-blue uniform, and glanced around. No one to meet us! Good. We could turn right around and catch the next train home!

"Coo-ee!" It was a tall thin woman with short chestnut hair, dumpling cheeks and a rosy apple face. For some reason she was wearing Wellington boots beneath a long black overcoat, which struck me as odd. She stepped forward, peering more closely at our cardboard labels.

"Fr-ank Car-ter. Vi-o-let Car-ter," she read slowly. "You're them!"

She held out a rough hand with dirty fingernails. "Mrs Grace Eleanor Pittaway." She spoke in a funny accent, like a pirate's wife.

"Come along-a me," she said over her shoulder, walking quickly from the station. Somehow I'd imagined a pony and trap waiting to take us to our new home. No such luck.

"Only three miles," said our new guardian.

Vi and I looked at each other in disbelief. Crikey! We'd never walked three miles in our lives. It wasn't long before we lagged behind the long-striding Mrs Pittaway. "Hurry up," she called impatiently. "I've got cows waiting on me."

We did our best. Down country lanes, past meadows of brown cows and woolly sheep, past mud heaps full of snorting, smudgy pink pigs. Whenever we passed anyone, they all seemed to know each other, shouting a greeting.

Violet, of course, has a big mouth and a nosey mind. "Did God make all those animals?"

"All things bright and beautiful, the Lord God made 'em all," shouted Mrs Pittaway, for all the world to hear.

"Fancy!" said Violet.

After a while, she asked, "Did he make Hitler too?"

Mrs Pittaway abruptly halted, hand over mouth.

"Hitler is Satan's handyman!" she cried, "sent to try us."

That was enough for a month of Sunday schools. Even Violet held her tongue after that.

Chapter Eleven

After about an hour, we arrived at Warren Farm, puffing and blowing, with muddy boots and soaking wet socks. But instead of standing before the front door, we were only at a wicket gate, with another long walk down a garden path to the green door of an old whitewashed thatched house. There was a sour-sweet smell in the air, very different from Grandad's sooty brushes.

"Take your shoes off!" ordered Mrs Pittaway.

We did as we were told, leaving my mucky boots and Vi's new shoes outside, before following the tall thin woman down a red-tiled passageway into the kitchen.

"Tha's milk in the churn," she said, taking off her coat and hat, and pulling on a green oilskin apron. "I got me cows waitin'. Hannah'll show you your room." With that she unlatched the back door and was gone.

"She's not very friendly," muttered my sister.

"P'raps farmers are like that," I said, "what with only pigs and cows to talk to."

We helped ourselves to milk with a long metal ladle from the milk churn by the back door. It was cold and creamy, nice and refreshing after our long

walk. Evidently milk wasn't rationed here.

"Cor, my feet are killing me," said Violet, imitating our mum. "I wonder who this Hannah is – her ladyship's maidservant or summat?"

"Yeah, milkmaid probably. Might be her daughter or cousin."

The back door suddenly burst open and a figure backed in, hauling a sackful of firewood. It obviously didn't notice us because, when I shifted my chair, scraping it on the stone floor, the back suddenly straightened up so quickly you'd think I'd said "Hands Up!"

A scared pale face whipped round, mouth open, brown hair flying, as the figure dropped the sack in the doorway. "Oh!"

"Sorry," I apologised. "I didn't mean to put the wind up you."

A girl of about my age stood staring at me, her hands shaking. Then, just as swiftly, she relaxed, her face wrinkling into a frosty smile. There was something about her I took an instant dislike to. I couldn't put my finger on it. Her face maybe – it was like a mask, hiding her true feelings. Or the way she held herself – proudly, as if we were below her. When she spoke, it was with a foreign accent, the words coming down her nose.

"You must be the 'vacuees," she said, "Violet and Frank. We've been expecting you."

She stuck out a hand for us to shake. "I'm Hannah, Hannah Kanel."

"You a foreigner?" asked Violet, with her usual tact.

"Er, no… er, yes. From Germany."

We both stiffened. "A German?"

It jumped out before I could stop it. More a dog's bark than a question. Her face turned a guilty red. "Er, no… er, yes."

Was she hiding something? Yes-no, no-yes. What was it?

"Are you a spy?" asked Violet, her eyes shining at the thought of meeting a real spy.

The girl ignored the question. Instead she changed the subject – obviously she *did* have something to hide!

"I'll show you your bedroom."

With that, she brushed past us, leading the way up the rickety stairs, over the first landing, up more stairs to an attic whose ceiling was so low we had to bow our heads. It smelt sweetly of hay and acorns. Hardly surprising, since one half of the wooden floor was covered in nuts.

"Walnuts," said Hannah, following our gaze. "They are drying out."

We'd only ever seen acorns. "Can you eat them?" asked Violet.

"Yes."

She must have thought better of it because she hastily added, "Ask Mrs Pittaway first, yes?"

She turned on her heel and hurried down the creaking stairway. We could hear her clip-clip-clopping over the kitchen tiles and out the back door – as if she wanted to get away as soon as possible.

"P'raps they're both German spies, Mrs Pittaway and her accomplice," hissed my sister.

"Don't be goofy, Vi," I said. "In the middle of the countryside? Farmers aren't like us townies. They're more, well, earthy. If you spend all day among baa-lambs and moo-cows, you probably get a bit like them."

Violet thought that over. "Mrs Pittaway looks a bit like a scrawny cow, doesn't she? She even smells of cow dung." I chuckled. "And that Hannah's like a dozy donkey with big brown eyes and big ears."

I jigged round the room, waggling my ears and eeh-awhing until we were both in stitches, collapsing on our beds beneath the rafters and skylight. The walk had tired us out, and poking fun at the two strangers cheered us up after all that had happened to us that day.

"Let's go and explore," I suggested, leaping up.

We collected our shoes and boots from outside the front door and sneaked round the side of the house, stopping at every corner and tree trunk to watch out for snipers. No one was about but chickens and ducks... and a dog sitting outside a kennel like a sentry before his pillbox. The instant he saw us, he lifted his nose to the heavens and sounded the alarm. He would surely have leapt up and torn out our throats had he not been chained to his kennel. He wasn't like our Bonzo, jumping up and licking your face.

We edged round the savage beast and ran, half crouching, for cover. Our noses led us to a big wooden barn at the side of the yard. A red-combed cockerel was strutting by, as if he owned the place. From the mooing and swishing of milk into pails we guessed this must be the cowshed.

What a stink! Our town noses weren't used to country smells. Violet and I held our noses as we trod carefully over the yard's cobblestones littered with wisps of straw, chicken poo and big squishy cowpats. I motioned to Vi to cover me as I peered into the shed. I could just make out the girl's figure sitting astride a three-legged stool, feeding a sweet little lamb with a baby's bottle.

Funny folk, these yokels, treating their animals like

humans! In wartime too. As we moved nearer for a closer look, a loud voice stopped us in our tracks. It was Mrs Pittaway.

"Make yerselves useful. Go collect up them eggs."

We darted back into the open. Eggs? What eggs? Where? We hadn't the foggiest idea where to start. Having made a hasty retreat, we gazed about us in search of hen and duck eggs. What else laid eggs? Pigeons? Pigs? Sheep?

"Better start with the chickens," I suggested.

"Where? They're all over the place," moaned my sister.

It was true. Some were pecking at bits of hay in the yard; some were under trees in the orchard at the back; some in the meadow chatting to sheep; a couple were standing on a big muck heap behind the kennel. One was pulling out the fattest worm I'd ever seen; even after losing its top half, the wriggly worm still squirmed.

Where *did* they hide their eggs? As luck would have it, the German spy came out, carrying two pails of milk.

"Where do we find eggs?" I asked civilly.

She stared at me as if I'd just landed from Mars. With a disdainful look, she pointed to a tumbledown little house beside the hay barn.

"Huh! Snotty-nosed madam!" I said when she'd gone.

"Do they expect us to go in there?" asked Vi, wrinkling her nose. "It looks full of creepy-crawlies. And it stinks."

"Think of the brave soldiers in the war!" I said with a laugh.

Leading the way past the wire netting of the chicken run, I unlatched the door and bent low into the chicken coop.

"Come on, Vi, looks like every animal has its own house on the farm," I muttered. "Cats, dogs, cows, chickens…"

"There's enough room in the country," she replied.

The smell inside the henhouse was like bad eggs mixed with sour milk. Our noses in our sleeves, we edged forward towards a shelf lined with straw.

"Hey, got one!" I shouted triumphantly. "And another."

Not to be outdone, my sister joined in, finding her own brown speckled eggs amidst the straw.

"This one's as warm as toast," she exclaimed. "Where we going to put them?"

We hadn't thought of that. There was no basket around, so I slipped the eggs into my trouser pockets until they were bulging.

"Better get them to the larder before they break or my pockets burst," I said.

As we backed out of the chicken run, we must have come within snip-snap range of the werewolf. I'd forgotten clean about him. All at once, he snapped at my heels, giving me such a fright I tripped over his chain and fell head first into the muck heap.

"You all right, Frank?" came a scared voice. It was Vi! She was obviously expecting to see a jagged bloody stump on the end of my leg.

"Think so," I murmured, feeling both ankles under my socks.

As I got to my feet gingerly, I suddenly felt something gooey trickling down my legs, as if I'd wet and pooed myself at the same time. The eggs! I'd forgotten all about them. And I didn't have any spare shorts to change into. It wasn't the best foot to start off on. And didn't Mrs Pittaway let me know it! For a god-fearing woman, she surprised us with her range of nasty names, some I'd never heard before: "Rapscallion! Scoundrel! Rascal! Clumsy oaf! Clot! I hates you all!" Even Hannah had got roped in. "Heathens! The lot o' ya. I never wanted ya in the first place. Thought it my Christian duty, so help me God! They billeted you on me..."

Chapter Twelve

Life among the cows and pigs was peaceful enough. No air raids. No shelter. No bombs or planes. No sirens to wake you in the middle of the night. Only the occasional splutter of excitement – like when a lone Jerry plane crash-landed nearby.

The Luftwaffe ace flying it must have bailed out or else melted into the ground. By the time we arrived after school, an area was roped off and debris was strewn about a black smoking crater. Vi and I went scouting round and came upon a little charred book. We knew it must be German because it was full of foreign words. The book was double Dutch to us – but we knew *someone* who spoke German.

Hannah kept herself to herself, sleeping in a cubbyhole off the first landing and getting up at the crack of dawn for milking and raking out the fire. True, the three of us walked the mile to school together every day. And we each had our sack to fill with rabbit food – dandelions, dock leaves, lamb's tails, clover. But prising a word out of her was like getting lambs to sing 'Baa-Baa Black Sheep'.

When she finished her chores in the evening, she'd squeeze into the corner nook beside the fire, staring into the dying flames. She'd screw up her eyes, clench

her fists and sometimes cry silent tears, turning away so that Mrs Pittaway didn't see. Our Mrs Pittaway, good woman that she was, didn't hold with wasting tears. She'd emptied hers into a hanky when her Bill had been killed in his very first battle.

"That's that," she once said. "No use crying over spilt milk. God's work has to be done."

In the middle of the night, Vi and I often heard sobbing coming from Hannah's room, and terrified shouts in some foreign tongue. As she said herself, the farmer's widow slept like a log, and it never woke her up.

When I asked Hannah what was wrong, she just kept silent, as if to say we'd been hearing things. Who was it we had heard crying then? A ghost?

There was something else that made us think she was round the twist. We heard her talking to someone in the milking shed! After the strange noises in the night, I thought we might discover clues as to what was going on. Was she just plain crazy, or was there a sinister plot we might uncover? Could there be a German spy hiding in the straw?

Excited at the thought of catching them in the act, Vi and I crouched down behind a hedge outside the shed hardly daring to breathe. We were too far away to overhear the whole conversation. Thrusting my

head forward and using both hands to clear twigs and leaves, I saw Hannah sitting on a stool with her back to us, milking a cow. There was no one else to be seen. She had to be talking to that black-and-white cow!

"She's cracked!" I hissed to Vi. "Would you credit it? She's talking away to the cow!"

"Perhaps it's a German dressed up as a cow?" suggested Vi seriously.

"Don't be daft, Vi," I muttered. But the thought of her talking to animals gave us both a fit of the giggles, and we almost gave the game away. When we'd simmered down, I again cocked an ear, seeing if I could recognize anything. A few scattered words reached me: *"Crystal… Nazi… Hans… violin…"*

What on earth did they mean? Did a Nazi called Hans play a crystal violin?! I told Vi and she couldn't stop laughing.

"Go on, Frank. What else does she say?" said Vi, tears of laughter running down her cheeks. I listened hard, but recognised no more words. She'd changed her tune and now, instead of cross words, her voice had softened to gentle mournful sighs: "Mama, Mama! Oh Papa, Papa, Papa!"

After the last 'Papa', she broke down and cried as if her heart would break.

"What's she saying, Frank?"

"Shush, Vi," I whispered with a catch in my throat. "I dunno what to make of it. She's crying for her mum and dad…"

"Oh."

"Come on, Sis," I said, feeling guilty. "Best leave her to it."

We slipped away quietly, none the wiser for our spying mission. Whatever secrets the girl was hiding, she obviously wasn't ready to share them with humans. Like it or not, however, she was the only one who could help us with our precious find. And since it might contain Jerry secrets, she *had* to help.

I stuck the book under her nose that evening as she was reading one of the house library books: *St George and the Dragon*. Since our find still reeked of smoke, she couldn't ignore it.

"Where did you find it?" she asked.

"Never you mind," I said, tapping my nose.

"Near the crashed plane," burst out Violet. "What's it say?"

A fine spy she'd make! Hannah turned a few pages, her brow knitted together like a rutted lane after a downpour.

"Well?"

There was no escape.

"It's called *What Are We Fighting For?* It's rubbish."

"Oh yeah," I drawled.

She sighed deeply, translating hesitantly.

"He who fights with the purest will, the strongest belief and the most fanatical determination will be victorious in the end…"

"Humph! Is that all?"

"It talks about Jews…"

"What's it say?"

"Kill them."

"What? Every Jew in the world?"

She must be making it up. I thought of little Sam Rubinstein. He might be a pain in the backside, but what had he done to get himself murdered?

"Hitler won't find any Jews in this neck of the woods," I said. "Up in London, maybe. But you don't get Jew boys down on the farm."

She caught her breath. "How about Jew girls?" she almost spat out. Her face had darkened and her black eyes were full of anger.

I laughed. I was just about to say something when it suddenly dawned on me… she was foreign. From Germany. She stuck up for Jews… she must have seen my face change, for abruptly she stood up and went off in a huff. Before she had reached the top of the stairs, she turned back and threw at me, "I'm a Jew girl!"

"Oh... sorry," I mumbled to her disappearing back. I felt bad.

After her footsteps had died away, Violet asked the predictable, "What's a Jew?"

I'd have liked to give her the benefit of my knowledge. But apart from Sam Rubinstein, I only knew about Jews and Israelites (were they the same?) from Sunday school and the odd comment from grown-ups.

"God's chosen people," I said, quoting our old vicar.

"Did he choose Hannah?"

"Must have."

"Why?"

"I dunno, do I? Maybe she's good at milking and he needs milkmaids for his heavenly cows."

Next day being Saturday, we had time to ourselves after our farm chores. One job we could mix with some fun was gathering rabbit food in the woods behind the farm. It gave us a chance to get out from under Mrs Pittaway's gaze, play games ('the Devil's invention', as our Guardian Angel put it!) like hide-and-seek, climb trees and pick violets and primroses.

The woods were magical and mysterious with the half-light filtering through the branches, casting shadows on fox-holes and gleaming eyes. The trees

– hazel and oak, beech and yew – were just coming into leaf. The woodland floor reeked with the malty smell of moss and bracken, and last year's leaves. Birdsong took me light years back to our backyard before the war – those chirpy chappies who whistled and warbled to remind us that spring was near.

"Vi, what d'ya reckon to a tiger hunt?" I said mid-morning.

"Wow-eee!" Her eyes lit up like tracer bullets.

"We'll take some sacks to stick them in. Put on your wellies in case we tread on a python's tail." My mind wandered from Tarzan to Hitler. "Who knows, we might just find some wreckage!"

She stared at me suspiciously. "Oh no, I'm not going into a bombed house again!"

"Yesterday's plane, stupid! We didn't actually see wreckage, did we? Just a blooming great crater; it could have been a bomb. We might find something *really* fantastic – like a Luger pistol, or an Iron Cross."

"Crumbs!"

Equipped for our adventure in wellies and farm dungarees, we headed for the 'deepest jungle'. Most people steered clear of this part of Nutbourne Woods. Its gnarled oaks and yews grew so densely you could barely glimpse the sky. But there was another reason:

some folk said the wood was haunted.

Now, in early April, the whiff of woody decay filled the air and the squelchy carpet of leaves gave off the mouldy smell of the grave. All at once, we caught the whiff of something else. Together, we lifted our noses and sniffed the air, trying to place it.

"What's that pong?" I whispered, wrinkling my nose.

"Phew-wer! Smells like burnt rubber or dead fireworks," said Vi, holding her nose. "Bit early for Bonfire Night."

It slowly dawned on us what the smell could mean. Nervously, we edged through the trees in silence, guided by the stench and gritty ash in nose and mouth. It was not long before we found what we were looking for.

A patch of grey-blue sky suddenly widened above a clearing. Twisted tree trunks reeled back, stripped of leafy cover. Snapped branches poked spindly white finger-bones at the open sky; and freshly dug brown soil lay upturned as if a legion of moles had been at work.

There before us, its nose buried deep in the earth, was an aeroplane. It was smaller than I expected. Perhaps that was because it was part-buried in the ground and the tail section and one wing had broken

off. The mangled tail lay in a black pool of mud and brackish water some distance from its body.

Vi let out a scream. She was evidently terrified by the stark black cross on the grey fuselage and the hated swastika on the broken tail. I was dead scared too, but I tried to put a brave face on it. After all, it was my idea to search for the crashed plane. And now we'd found it, we deserved to take our reward.

I squeezed my sister's hand.

"It's okay, Vi," I said in hushed tones. "A crashed plane can't hurt you. Come on, let's take a look. Maybe we'll find those goggles you've always wanted."

But Vi was rooted to the spot. "C-c-can you s-s-see any dead bodies?" she stuttered.

I plucked up courage and stepped warily towards the main section of the plane. I had to hold a hanky to my nose; even now patches of fuel were smouldering all around and filling the air with an awful stink.

Chapter Thirteen

If I stood on tiptoe, I could just peer into the cockpit through the cracked perspex window. All I could make out was a charred mass; it could be anything. If there was a dead body in there, it was unrecognizable.

"Can't see a darn thing," I told Vi. "No sign of the pilot."

"Come on, Frank," she squeaked nervously. "Let's get out of here."

I too was starting to feel queasy. The entire petrol-soaked glade could go up in flames at any moment. As I went to grab Vi's arm to pull her away, however, we both froze in terror.

From the dark wood came a muffled groan. It was a most terrible, ghostly sound, "Ai-aiyai-ai-ai! Oh-oo-oo-oo!"

We hugged each other in sheer panic, too scared to move. I felt the hair on the back of my neck bristling, like that of a frightened dog. Vi started to cry, softly, so as not to alert the monster.

"Ooo-ooo-hhh! Ohh-hhh-ohh!"

"What's that?" squeaked Vi.

I just wanted to grab her and run all the way back to the farm. But I forced myself to stay calm, even though my heart was racing like an express train and

I was quaking in my wellies. Whatever happened, I had to keep calm.

"Don't panic!" I squawked. "Someone's in pain, wounded – maybe dying."

Like Hansel and Gretel, we advanced slowly, hand in hand, one step at a time. We moved towards a dense copse. But it wasn't a house of gingerbread that stood before us. It was a giant mushroom. The mushroom's white top was tangled in the treetops, so that its stalk was now swinging to and fro, head-high above the forest floor. Here was our ghost!

He was dressed in navy blue overalls, and had long brown boots and a grey leather flying helmet on his head. His eyes were closed, and strands of fair hair were stuck to his brow. Blood had dried beneath his nose and ears, and at the corners of his mouth.

"Is he… is he… dead?" asked Vi, so quietly I could scarcely hear.

"Not as long as he's groaning," I said with a grim smile. "Dead men don't groan. Mind you, if he stays like this much longer, he'll most likely choke on his own blood."

"We must do something," whispered Vi. "We can't just leave him to die. It'll take hours to fetch help."

I gave her a grumpy look. "Whose side are you

on?" I said crossly. "Why should we help a German? We didn't ask him to bomb us!"

But Vi was stubborn. "What if Dad fell into German hands? We'd hope that if kids found him, they'd do what they could to save his life, wouldn't we?"

I ignored her; I was thinking. "I suppose he might have secrets," I muttered, half to myself. "The police could winkle them out of him."

I made up my mind. "Grab his legs while I try to unhook the 'chute'."

It was easier said than done. At first we tried yanking and tugging his legs and arms, first one way, then the other. But that only tightened the noose around his neck.

"Go easy, Frank," yelled Vi. "You're strangling him."

"No less than he deserves," I grunted.

After a pause, I relented. "Oh, hold on. I suppose I'll have to risk my neck."

Hitching up my baggy dungarees, I reached up and swung myself into the tree which held the harness. I stuck first one foot into a cleft, then the other, until I'd climbed up to the branch supporting the harness. I crawled along the branch, my feet and thighs gripping the tree, grazing knees and elbows in the process. Then I set to unravelling the parachute.

It was slow, painstaking work, rather like trying to unknot a tangled fishing line. At last I called down, my words coming in puffs and pants,

"Hold on… tight… to his… f-f-feet."

I unhooked one last cord and, with a tearing crash, the body slumped to the ground, knocking Vi over and half smothering her.

As for me, the branch sprang sharply upwards, leaving me dangling in the air, high above the ground. I was left holding on by my toes and one hand.

There was nothing for it but to drop and hope for the best. With a despairing "Here I come!" I went sprawling in a heap. At once I felt a sharp pain in my right ankle.

"Ouch! I almost ended up killing myself to save his miserable skin!"

Painfully, I picked myself up and stepped gingerly towards Vi. I pulled her free from under the body before turning my attention to the unconscious German. Together we laid him on his back upon the leafy soil.

He was still breathing, though his breath was coming in short gasps. He looked half dead already. We needed to keep him alive if only for interrogators to force secrets out of him. Vi was right: it could take hours for those old fogies in the Home Guard to get

here on their bikes. What was needed was someone to talk to him in his own lingo, find out how bad his injuries were, get some sense out of him. Hannah! While I stood guard over the prisoner, I sent Vi back to the farm.

"Run like mad, Vi. Lives could depend on you. Bring Hannah back urgently!"

She took ages. I imagined Vi arguing with Hannah; I knew she wouldn't fancy coming face to face with a German. Odd that: if I'd been in Jerryland and come upon an English pilot, we'd have got on very well.

But these two Germans... it wasn't exactly love at first sight when Hannah finally arrived. I told her straight. "As Mrs Pittaway would say, 'needs must where the Devil drives'. It's our duty to keep the prisoner alive and learn what we can from him, *if we are to win the war.*"

I left her to it, with Vi as referee if they tried to scratch each other's eyes out. Meanwhile, I limped off to the police station at Emsworth, a couple of miles away. God knows what Hannah and the pilot talked about. By the time I got back with a squad of Home Guards, two Bobbies and an ambulance woman, our prisoner was sitting up.

From the look of relief on his face, he was obviously glad to get away from his fellow German.

Chapter Fourteen

That was that: the last we heard of our prisoner. First thing Monday morning, we handed in our 'find' – the German book – to Miss Hopkinson. Since she didn't speak Jerry lingo either, she invited Hannah to translate for us.

But Hannah refused to talk about the German book. To our surprise, Miss Hopkinson didn't punish her. Instead of flying off the handle, the teacher said softly, "I understand."

She never said that to me when I got my sums wrong or couldn't tell her where Tobruk was on our wall map. "Never mind, Hannah," she said. "I'm sure we *all* understand."

Blowed if I understood anything when it came to Hannah. The frosty attitude. The sounds at night. The odd words and tears for Betsy the cow. Something was going on, but the more I thought about this strange girl, the more questions I had.

At milk break, someone must have whispered in Miss Hopkinson's ear because she went and gave us a sermon on 'refugees'.

"Adolf Hitler is our enemy," she began. "Why is he our enemy? Yes, Charlie."

"'Cos he bombs us, Miss."

"That's right. He kills British people. I know some of you evacuees have lost loved ones because of Mr Hitler and his Nazis. Now... whom did Mr Hitler start by killing?" Two hands shot up.

"Australians, Miss!"

"No, Faye. I expect you mean 'Austrians'. Yes, he attacked Austria. But before Austria, he was killing his own people."

That surprised us.

"What for, Miss?" asked Barbara, who shared a desk with me.

"Hands up if you want to ask a question!" said the teacher sternly. "Margaret? Why did he kill his own people?"

"To eat them, Miss?"

Before any more daft answers could follow, she waved hands down. "I'll tell you why. To get to power he had to defeat the communists. So they were the first group he murdered. That didn't satisfy him. He looked round for poor handicapped people. You see, he wants a strong, pure race of Aryans."

She didn't bother asking for a show of hands on *Aryans*. But one hand did go up; to our surprise it was Hannah at the back. Normally, she *never* volunteered an answer to anything. Now she was giving an answer *before* the question!

"Yes, Hannah? Can you tell us what an Aryan is?"

"Someone who's not Jewish, Miss."

"Well, to Hitler an Aryan is anyone who's not Jewish. But really Aryan is a language of the Indo-European family. It dates back to the Hittites over two thousand years ago. So Aryan, you see, children, is a *language*, not a *race* as Mr Hitler claims."

Her gaze swept round the class to ensure we all took it in. But she wasn't finished. "Now, Hannah, you're Jewish, aren't you? Tell me, what's your native language?"

"German, Miss Hopkinson."

"Is that an Aryan language, class?"

Nodding heads confirmed it.

"Yes, it is. That's correct. Do you speak any other languages, Hannah? Besides English, I mean."

All heads swivelled round to take a new look at Hannah. She fidgeted uncomfortably in her chair and slowly put her hand up.

"Yes, go on. Go on, girl."

"No, but some of my relatives spoke Yiddish, before the war. It's a dialect of German. But... the Rabbi at the synagogue spoke Hebrew, so my cousin Erich told me. None of us spoke it at home."

Miss Hopkinson rubbed her hands, warming to her task. Turning to the class, she asked,

"Is Yiddish an Aryan language if it's like German?"

"Yes, Miss," we chimed back.

"How about Hebrew? Think carefully."

That had us. Even Hannah didn't seem to know.

"Hebrew is a very old language, spoken in ancient Palestine for over a thousand years. It's a strange language, written from right to left – back to front, so to speak." She held up a book and traced a finger from the right side of the page to the left. "And it's made up entirely of consonants. It isn't like English at all; so it's non-Aryan."

"No wonder it died out," I whispered. "How can you pronounce a word with no vowels?"

Turning round, the teacher said, "The Bible was written in Hebrew. Jesus, after all, was a Jew."

I felt my face reddening. Jews like Hannah were responsible for our Bible; and, if Hitler was against the Jews, she was on *our* side… and we had to be on *her* side.

"Your family's still in Germany, isn't it?" asked Miss Hopkinson.

Hannah's head was bent over her desk, as if she didn't want to answer. As the clock ticked on loudly, Miss Hopkinson seemed to realize she'd pushed Hannah too far.

"I'm sorry. I didn't mean to pry."

Right then the clanging of the school bell announced the end of the lesson. We all jumped up. But the schoolmistress's stern tones "Wait!" froze us like marble statues.

"Hannah has her hand up. Sit down, all of you. Yes, Hannah."

In a very quiet voice, she said, "Hitler drove my family out of our home. I've had no word from them."

You could have heard a pin drop. The class sat there stunned. How? A little peep came from Barbara beside me:

"Why?"

"Because we are Jews…"

Once she got her teeth into something, Miss Hopkinson wouldn't let go. Next day, after prayers, instead of doing our times table and a spelling test, she announced a history lesson. But, would you believe? She asked us to imagine we were Germans!

I didn't fancy that at all. Jerry kids sick hiling all over the shop, being bred to fight us and bomb us to bits. If I'd had the courage, I'd have told her Jerries killed my Uncle Jack, and Maisie and Eric Eddles. But I kept quiet, deciding to stay English in my head.

The only one who knew about being German was Hannah – since she was German. She had to stand at

the front and treat us to tales of her schooldays. I did my best to close my ears; it wasn't right to listen to that sort of talk. Mind you, after all the crying of yesterday and stuff about her family, most of the class seemed eager to ask questions about her school friends and teachers.

I was shocked. The more I heard, the more sorry for her I was. Fancy having to put up with that. How cruel! How could they treat little children like animals? A far cry from the sort of bullying I'd seen at school: making fun of fatties, like podgy Jessup. No, no, that wasn't in the same league. That had been just a bit of harmless fun.

The bit that really got to me was when she told us about her birthday party, when she was eleven. She'd invited six children, including her best friend. But no one came. I must admit, I had a lump in my throat as Hannah finished the story. Poor girl! What a terrible thing to happen. On your birthday too.

I pictured myself in Germany. The question nagging at me was whose side would I have been on? In my mind's eye I could clearly see little Sam Rubinstein. To my shame I remembered how I'd taunted him, joined in with others to call him 'Jew boy!' Why had I disliked him so? Yes, I know why. I'd hated Sam Rubinstein because *others* hated him. I'd

hated him so much I could have punched him on the nose. But why? He'd never done me any harm. He always tried to be friendly.

I needed time to think this out. My brain, my heart, they were all jumbled up. I wanted to run away and hide. Better still, go back and start all over again, not only with Hannah. I felt like going back to London to find Sam and tell him how sorry I was. For the moment, I couldn't look Hannah in the eye.

Chapter Fifteen

Mrs Pittaway had no wireless. "Devil's invention!" she claimed. "If God meant us to have wireless, He'd have given us an extra sense." She read no newspaper either, apart from *Parish News,* which reported on births, deaths and miracles.

So all we knew about the war came from Miss Hopkinson's wall map and Mum's letters. Most scraps of information were about faraway, exotic-sounding places: Trincomalee, Tripoli, El Alamein, Stalingrad, Kursk... Perhaps the government was trying to hide disasters in Europe, though Mussolini got kicked out of Italy. Everyone knew the Italians weren't much good at war.

Mum's promise to visit us was a long time in the keeping. She arrived by train, but only stayed a couple of hours – "Have to get back before black-out," she said.

Mrs Pittaway and Hannah were out working on the farm so we had some private time together. The three of us were sitting round the table in the kitchen. Mum came out with it. "I've some bad news."

We knew at once that someone had died. But who? Gran? Grandad? Neighbours? It could be anyone with those bombs flying about. With a toss of

her head, she quickly said, "Gran passed away. Peacefully. In her sleep. She's at rest now…"

Vi and I cried. We loved Gran as much as she loved us. It was hard to imagine her no longer lying on the front room couch, next to the aspidistra plant.

"She sent you her love before… you know, before she passed on. We had a really nice funeral last Monday; you can see the grave and flowers from our front-bedroom window."

Mum herself had a bout of the sniffles. But… it sounded like she was trying to get something else out through her sobs.

"Not… all… be brave, chil…"

We could see that a lump in her throat was blocking her words. Then, with a painful swallow, they flew out on a rush of air.

"Your dad's been killed."

We stared at her, uncomprehending. I felt numb like I'd never felt before. Mum slowly told us the story.

"A long brown envelope arrived last Tuesday, after Gran's funeral. It had my name on it: Kathleen May Carter. The letter was waiting for me on the table when I got home from work… propped up against the cocoa tin. I knew what it was straightaway. "Harold's dead!" I said quietly. It was all very formal:

your dad's details filling the spaces: 'A report has been received from the War Office…Private Albert Harold Carter… 5th Hants… listed as missing. Presumed dead… 15th Day of May 1942'."

She took the letter from her handbag and passed it to me, carefully, as if it was her most treasured possession. I read it aloud. For a few moments, we were all silent. Not even a sniff. "It doesn't *say* he's dead," said Vi in a tiny voice. "Just missing. He might have got lost."

We both looked up at Mum, waiting for her answer, clinging on to hope.

"'Missing' means they didn't find his body, see. They wouldn't say 'presumed dead' if they thought he was alive."

Mum sipped her tea quietly, then burst into tears, burying her face in her hands. Vi and I cried and cried. Mum stayed with us for another hour. We talked about Dad, cried a lot more, but I still couldn't get rid of that numb feeling. I remembered the day Dad got his call-up papers right before the war really started – I thought it sounded like a bit of a holiday for him. For a second I felt angry – then the sadness came flooding back. At last, Mum dried her eyes and stood up.

"I'll come and see you soon. Must be on my way,

must get back before blackout." She kissed us both and quickly left, dabbing her eyes.

We were left alone with our grief: first Gran, then Dad. It was too much. We wanted our mum. Yet when we needed her most she wasn't there.

Hannah was the first to come in, lugging a milk churn. For once, she was in a happy mood. Yet when she saw our tear-stained faces and red eyes, her smile swiftly faded.

"Our gran's died. Dad's been killed." Vi came right out with it.

Hannah went as white as a sheet, then her bottom lip quivered and tears rolled down her cheeks – as if it were *her* grandmother and father.

"Oh, how dreadful. I'm so sorry," she said. "Poor Violet. Poor Frank."

She fell to her knees, put her arms round my neck and pulled my head on to her shoulder. She did the same to Vi, kissing her wet cheeks. And all three of us were crying. After a few minutes, she helped us up, saying, "Come, go for a walk in the fields. It'll make you feel better. Meanwhile, I'll break the news to Mrs Pittaway."

We put up no resistance, following her dumbly out into the yard and making for the meadows beyond the farm. When we got back, Mrs Pittaway had a

baked sago pudding on the table waiting for us. I guess that was her way of expressing her sympathy.

Following quickly after our terrible news, we had a visit. Around dinner time the following Sunday, two men in long black coats pulled up in a shiny black motor car, a Riley. Any car was an event in the country; we were more used to bikes, wheelbarrows, horses and carts.

We were in the middle of saying grace. Mrs Pittaway had got as far as 'For what we are about to receive, may the Lord make us truly thankful'. What we received was not what we expected.

A loud knocking echoed through the house. Mrs Pittaway marched up the passage to see who it was. When she returned she had these two tall men with her. They must have been important because she hadn't even made them remove their shoes.

"Hannah Kanel!" (he pronounced it *Canal*), demanded one in a loud voice.

Hannah looked up. Her eyes stared as if she was facing the executioner; her voice trembled as she said,

"Yes. That's me."

"Stay where you are!"

I expected the next words to be "I've got you covered!" But he said matter-of-factly, "This won't take long." And he stood with his backside to the fire,

glaring from one to the other of us as if we were all in it together.

Meanwhile, the other man trod heavily up the stairs accompanied by Mrs Pittaway. We could hear him stamping on the floorboards above our heads, pulling open drawers and chucking things on the floor.

"What in heaven's name is going on?" asked Mrs Pittaway in a shrill voice as they came back downstairs. "I demand an explanation."

"We've received certain information," said the man warming his bottom, "that leads us to believe that this girl," he pointed a long finger at Hannah, "is... transmitting secrets to the enemy."

Secrets? What secrets? How many rabbits we have?

'Transmitting secrets' didn't satisfy Mrs Pittaway. She must have thought they were talking about some religious paper, like the Salvation Army *War Cry*. "We each have our own God. Hannah is a good, hard-working girl. I'll swear on the Bible to that."

The man sneered, ignoring her. Just then his companion clattered down the stairs and entered, shaking his head. One of them said to Hannah, "Collect your things! You're coming with us!"

All manner of thoughts flashed through my head. Maybe Hitler was right about the Jews if the British Secret Service thought them dangerous. But...

Hannah was on our side. She wasn't a spy. She couldn't be, could she?

We watched from the doorway as they bundled her into the car, clutching her worldly possessions in a tiny bag. She didn't cry: all her tears must have been used up. Vi wept for her as the motor car sped away.

I felt wretched. I went into the yard to kick some straw and pour out my troubles to Rufus, the guard dog. Now it was my turn to talk to the animals.

"'Tain't fair," I told him. "Poor girl. Alone without her family. Now this."

Rufus seemed to understand. Instead of baring his teeth, he laid his head on his paws, gazing sadly up at me, listening to my every word, and whimpering.

We both felt sorry – for her and for ourselves. I hadn't had a chance to apologize properly for being spiteful. Nor had I said what I wanted about being rude. I just couldn't find the words. Many's the time I wanted to say how sorry I was for her family. But I never did.

Would I have another opportunity?

Now flip over and read
Hannah's side of the story!